THE SECRETS OF DROON

THE FINAL QUEST

A Magical World Awaits You
Read

THE
SECRETS
OF
DROON

THE FINAL QUEST

TONY ABBOTT

ILLUSTRATED BY ROYCE FITZGERALD
COVER ILLUSTRATION & MAP BY TIM JESSELL

SCHOLASTIC INC.
New York Toronto London Auckland
Sydney Mexico City New Delhi Hong Kong

For Dolores, Jane, and Lucy
and our Long Story Together

For more information about the epic saga of Droon,
please visit Tony Abbott's website at
www.tonyabbottbooks.com

ISBN 978-0-545-09885-4

Text copyright © 2010 by Tony Abbott.
Illustrations copyright © 2010 by Scholastic Inc.

All rights reserved. Published by Scholastic Inc.
SCHOLASTIC, LITTLE APPLE, and associated logos
are trademarks and/or registered trademarks of Scholastic Inc.

12 11 10 9 8 7 6 5 4 3 2 1   10 11 12 13 14 15/0

Printed in the U.S.A.   40
First printing, October 2010

Contents

One

The Half Prophecy

"Look there beyond those dunes," the dragon told his rider. "Another fire. Another victory."

As Gethwing's four enormous wings, black and ragged as ripped fabric, lifted him high over the world of Droon, Eric Hinkle forced himself to look down.

Beneath the twisting plumes of smoke below stood a tiny village cradled among vast dunes of sand. Until it had been abandoned and burned, the village had been the home of the purple Lumpies and their beloved ruler, Khan.

Eric's heart ached as they swooped low over the crumbled huts, and then soared high again.

Beyond the desert village, he spied a range of hilltop settlements sprinkled among the Dust Hills of Panjibarrh. Also in flames, also uninhabited, they were all that remained of the Oobja people's royal homeland.

"Good work," Eric managed to say, nearly choking on the words. "Really nice."

"Indeed," Gethwing said, banking so sharply over a range of pink mountains that Eric had to cling to the dragon's horns to keep from falling. "A great day shall soon dawn for me, and for you, Prince Ungast."

Prince Ungast! Eric thought disgustedly. *How I hate that name!*

Not long before, Eric had been wounded, cursed, and transformed into his evil twin, Prince Ungast.

Though he had been cured, Eric had stayed in disguise, hoping to bring down Gethwing from within the dragon's beast-filled ranks.

Now only Ungast's ill-fitting purple armor

stood between him and Gethwing's terrifying wrath.

"More fires!" the dragon said, swooping over a string of burning villages. "Our war is nearly complete. Soon, we enter the final day."

Gethwing's ultimate battle against Eric's beloved Droon was only three and a half days old, but already fires had destroyed its major cities, and heaps of rubble were all that remained of great palaces.

Knowing that a scant thirty hours remained until the predicted final siege on Jaffa City, Eric was frantic to stop the dragon.

If Gethwing could be stopped at all.

In the last few hours Eric had learned that the dragon was not simply a monster possessing power rooted in Droon's earliest days.

Gethwing was much more.

Gethwing was . . . *immortal*.

"And there," the dragon said. "Let us take a closer look at that lovely . . . destruction."

As if drawing a map of invisible lines from one conquest to the next, Gethwing veered away from the pink mountains to a valley clouded by the densest smoke.

"Such fine flames," murmured the dragon. "Don't you think, Ungast?"

"Oh, you bet," Eric said.

At first, Eric had been stunned to learn that Droon's enemy could not die. But it made sense. Countless times over his long life, Gethwing had been attacked, wounded, cursed, thought near death, and yet each time the Moon Dragon had escaped his end.

The reason was simple.

According to Eric's genie friend, Neal Kroger, Gethwing could never be defeated as long as his mysterious "wheel of life" continued to spin.

Fine, thought Eric. *So he's got a wheel.*

Except that Gethwing's wheel was hidden in a place called the Cave of Night, and no one knew where that was.

Still worse, Neal had learned that there was an ancient prophecy proving that Gethwing would never die, that he would rule forever.

As part of his big push to conquer Droon, the dragon had formed his Crown of Wizards — uniting under him the powers of the sorcerer Lord Sparr, the wickedly clever Princess Neffu, and Prince Ungast.

As long as the dragon believed Eric to be his second in command, the boy could work undercover to defeat him before Jaffa City — and all of Droon — fell.

All I have to do is discover the prophecy. Stop the wheel. Defeat Gethwing. End the war. Not much. Just that.

Summoning his courage, Eric spoke.

"So listen, Gethwing, the big battle. How exactly will the whole thing happen —"

"Hush!" snarled the dragon. "Look there!"

Gethwing banked over what had once been the diamond-strewn Kalahar Valley — before a hundred thousand beast hooves had trampled it to little more than a barren wasteland.

"Not bad, eh, Ungast?" asked Gethwing, arching his head back at Eric. "My armies — *our* armies — are but hours away from complete victory in Droon. If the Forbidden City of Plud will be my new capital, perhaps Jaffa City can be yours. How does . . . Ungast Town sound to you?"

Eric's throat tightened, his stomach turned. *Ungast Town!* Then he realized something. Plud had long been Lord Sparr's home. In fact, it was one of the very first places Eric and his friends had ever visited in Droon. If Gethwing now wanted Plud for himself . . .

Eric suddenly sensed a second crack in the fearful Crown of Wizards.

"Plud, huh?" he said. "But what about Lord Sparr? Plud has always been his favorite city."

"Sparr?" said Gethwing, soaring up again. "Sparr will join us after he finishes his siege of Zorfendorf Castle. And Neffu will meet us after her victory over the port of Doobesh."

Eric tamped down his anger again.

Doobesh was a city ruled by King Jabbo. The pie-making king was one of many souls — thousands of them — loyal to Droon.

But good souls were not enough.

Eric knew that he and his friends could do only so much. His dream had long been to reunite the three sons of Zara, the Queen of Light. Only Galen, Urik, and Sparr together possessed the depth of magic needed to stop the dragon.

Yet Eric was aware that this was an impossible dream.

Zara had passed away centuries ago, Galen was missing, and Urik was lost in the sunless depths of time. Bringing them together, uniting them once more, was clearly impossible.

That leaves only Sparr, he thought. *I need to turn him to our side. I have to make him join his magic to ours! We need more magic. We need as much magic as possible!*

The dragon circled a nearby mountaintop and lighted on its barren peak.

An outcropping below was sprinkled with the remains of a groggle nest. Groggles were the flying lizards preferred by beasts. One old creature lay sleeping there. The others, Eric guessed, had all been recruited for the war.

"You can see much from here," the dragon said, tucking his wings behind him.

Eric slid from the dragon's scaly back to solid ground. It was difficult to do anything without Gethwing realizing it, since the dragon was as clever and brilliant as he was powerful. Yet Eric wondered if he could wrench a clue from Gethwing without seeming to.

"So . . . ," he began.

"Ungast," said the dragon, letting his eyes play over Eric's face. "Prince . . . son . . ."

The word made Eric tremble, but he caught himself and turned away, lest the quaking of his chest inside his breastplate betray his fear.

"Dad," he said with a smirk.

"You jest," said the dragon. "I do not. These next hours will cement our lordship over Droon. There are secrets about me that no one knows. Neffu and Sparr are essential to this attack, yes —"

"Sparr," said Eric, seizing on the name and removing his helmet. "I've been meaning to talk to you about him."

"Yes?" said the dragon.

"It's just that Sparr has gone back and forth, hasn't he?" said Eric. "I mean, sure, since we started the Crown of Wizards, he's been working hard to help us conquer Droon. But sometimes, well, you know, he goes back to *them*. The kids. He helps them. He's kind of a question mark."

Gethwing kept his eyes on Eric's face. "Is he?"

"Maybe I should check on him," Eric said, averting his gaze. "Make sure he's with us. For the final attack."

Gethwing glanced toward the horizon in the far west. The sun was setting, its final rays as red as blood. "Like a good boy checks on an aging relative. How touching."

"I mean, I don't want to," said Eric, trying not to show eagerness. "I just think I should fly over to Zorfendorf and see how his siege is coming along. To keep an eye on him. Make sure he's with us."

Gethwing nodded. "Of course, of course. My Crown of Wizards is vital for our victory."

For a few moments, as the sun dipped below the sea and the sky flared redder than red, no one spoke.

"But afterward?" said Gethwing finally. "On the field of victory, some thirty short hours from now? Not all shall remain. I know this because of . . . because of an ancient prophecy."

So? You want to talk about it? Then let's talk.

"You've never told me about a prophecy," said Eric, as casually as he could. "So I really wouldn't know."

Gethwing took Eric's gloved hands in his own enormous claws. "The words were spoken on the night of my birth. They were inscribed in stone that very hour. After centuries, those words are now being fulfilled."

The dragon paused, staring into Eric's eyes. *"Five shall pass away, four shall wear the crown, three shall fall, two shall rise together..."*

Silently memorizing the words, Eric waited, but the dragon said no more.

"Interesting," Eric said. "But what about the *one*? Isn't there something cool about the *one*?"

"The five that shall pass away," Gethwing said, dismissing his question, "are the cycles of Droon's millennial calendar. Five have come and gone since I first breathed. The four that shall wear the crown? These are the four in the Crown of Wizards — Sparr, Neffu, you, and me. I formed the Crown because of the prophecy."

Okay. That makes sense. Go on...

"Of the three that shall fall," Gethwing said, "Emperor Ko and Queen Zara are two of them. Ko fell to his death. Zara has long since passed away and lies entombed."

Zara! Why you —

Eric suppressed an urge to strike Gethwing with his sword. "And the *two* and the *one*?"

"Of the *one*," the dragon murmured, "let us simply say that it speaks of the end of days, and burning and ashes, and, well, you will know soon, Ungast. The world will know soon. Both worlds! Far more interesting are the *two that shall rise together*. For they are standing on this mountaintop right now."

A surge of excitement coursed through Eric's veins, but when it fizzled in an instant, he knew that Ungast was truly a thing of the past. "But really. What about the one?"

Gethwing's jaws twisted into a smile, but there was a flicker of uncertainty in his eyes. "All will be known when the time comes."

Really? thought Eric. *Are you telling me that you don't actually know what the prophecy means? Seriously? That's like only knowing half of it. Then, good! What happens to "the one" will be a surprise to all of us — especially to you, dragon!*

An icy wind swept across the mountaintop, and Eric hunkered down in his armor.

"Get used to it," Gethwing said, his eyes scouring the passes below. "We will walk in a place far colder than this before the final day is over." Gethwing waved his claws wide.

A place far colder than this? Is that a clue?

"Until then, take this," said the dragon, slipping a studded bracelet over Eric's wrist. "Use it during these final hours. Use it against your enemies. Including those you think are closest to you."

"But I'm only going to see Sparr," said Eric. "There's no danger of enemies."

"Nevertheless," said Gethwing, removing his claws from the bracelet.

The thick band was freezing cold and felt like nothing so much as ice carved into a twisted length of black stone.

"Stylish," said Eric.

Gethwing nodded slowly. "I have used it in the past to alert me to betrayers. Use it even against Sparr, if you must. Remember, only

you and I shall rise together. Only we two are essential after this war is over."

So you're giving Sparr the boot?

I can use that.

Eric grinned as evilly as he could. "Thanks for the jewelry."

Eric turned to the south. Zorfendorf Castle was no more than a speck of white among the far hills, catching the last flickers of daylight.

"I'll be back," he said.

"I know you will," said Gethwing. "I know. Until then, find out about Sparr. Let him share his secrets with you. Be his friend. Go."

It was the dragon's last word to him.

As he watched Gethwing fly off, Eric thought he had held his own against him. *Gethwing doesn't suspect me, does he? I don't think so. He even gave me a weapon. A magic bracelet. Yeah, well, I'll turn it against you, Gethwing, the first chance I get. Now . . . to fool Sparr. In a different way.*

He climbed down to the groggle nest, reached the creature sleeping there, and woke it. Lumbering to its feet, the lizard knew from the evil cast of Eric's armor to obey his commands.

Leaping onto the lizard's rough back, Eric grabbed the long fins on its head and gave it a nudge with his heels.

The final war? The ashes of the old world?

His blood ran cold as the creature soared over the smoky plains, beating its wings noisily toward the white-walled castle of Zorfendorf.

Two

War of the Words

Though the groggle flew high into the icy air, it wasn't cold that caused Eric to wrap his cloak tightly around him. The trembling in his side came from another source.

Pushing his hand inside his cloak, Eric loosed the magical Medallion from his pocket. Holding it again, he could not stop its strange story from flooding into his mind, for in a way it was the Moon Medallion that held the entire history of his adventures in Droon.

Created centuries before by Zara, the Medallion was constructed of four parts, one made by Zara and each of her three sons, Sparr, Galen, and Urik.

Zara's base was called the Silver Moon; the Ring of Midnight was crafted by Galen; the Twilight Star by Sparr; and the Pearl Sea by Urik.

It was when following Sparr to Pesh, the ancient city of the thorn queen, Salamandra, that Eric had first learned the story of Zara. Founder of a dynasty of powerful wizards, Zara was as kind as she was just. Envy of her powerful magic caused the fierce, bull-headed Emperor Ko to enter the Upper World and kidnap her.

When Sparr escaped from Salamandra through her thorny time portal, Urik followed him and was lost in an endless loop of time. Galen then used Urik's magical wand to create the rainbow-colored staircase and search for his kidnapped mother.

It was the discovery of that magical staircase that first brought Eric and his friends to Droon.

Hiding the Medallion in his cloak once more, Eric knew that in its intricate markings were millions of words that formed nothing less than a history of universal magic.

How many times since coming to Droon had Eric learned how words and names carried power beyond belief: Salamandra, Pesh, Urik, the Dark Lands, Jaffa City, Doobesh, Gethwing, Zorfendorf, Sparr, Ko, the Forbidden City of Plud, Zara!

And now more words!

Five shall pass away . . .

Even as Eric's brain crowded with the vast mystery of all things, his heart ached with uncertainty. What does it all mean?

But I still have to try to save Droon, don't I? There are less than thirty hours to discover the prophecy, Gethwing's mysterious wheel of life, and the dark secret that will stop him.

The groggle dipped from the purpling sky, and the boy saw row upon row of red-faced and black-armored Ninn warriors crowding the fields below. Some pushed a giant war tower, while others hauled a battering ram in the shape of a dragon's head.

"If only my friends were here," he said.

If only. But Keeah, Neal, and Julie were needed elsewhere, fighting one of the countless other battles, doing their best to stave off the final war Eric feared they had already lost.

He slowed the groggle with a nudge of his heels, and it landed atop a nearby hill. He slipped from its back, scoured the fields below, and saw the man he had come to find.

Lord Sparr was mounted on a winged black pilka. Mantled in a long gray cloak, the sorcerer gazed motionless at the tumult of battle, the fins behind his ears bloodred in the twilight. All of a sudden, Sparr stood in his stirrups and shouted. "The eastern wall is breached! Ninns, batter the twin gates now!"

Eric gulped. "This is the guy I'm hoping to

bring to my side? I may need this bracelet after all." He twisted the cold black band up his arm, hiding it inside his cloak. He hoped that Sparr would sense neither it nor the Moon Medallion.

Leaping down from his pilka, Sparr suddenly called, "Ungast! A surprise visit. Come. Enter the city with us!"

Eric secured his war helmet. It felt heavier than ever. "Coming!" he said.

Rushing to join Sparr, Eric spied groups of inhabitants streaming from rough openings in the walls and escaping into the scrubby margins of the nearby woods. There were many small children among them, their little cheeks smudged with the grime of battle except where they were marked by tears.

He wished he could tell them who he really was. But to these children, *pretending* to be bad must seem the same as *being* bad.

I'll make it up to them later. I promise —

Blam! Blam! After two strokes of the battering ram, the city's white gates fell inward, and the sorcerer leaped through. "Ninns, Ungast, follow me!"

Together with his warriors, Sparr charged his way into the castle yard. Without pause, he left his troops, raced across the yard, and tore open an iron-studded door with a wave of his hand.

"Where are you going?" Eric called.

Sparr said nothing, but rushed into the darkness of the castle. He continued without stopping, through corridors, this way and that, straight to the royal library.

Entering the high-ceilinged room with Sparr, Eric heard a hushed fluttering of wings near the uppermost bookshelves. Three disheveled birds had lighted up there and peered down. *Poor frightened creatures*, he thought. *Maybe birds will be the only ones to survive this war. Maybe not even them.*

Sparr did not stop. He tore across the library to a far door, whispered a word, and disappeared through it.

The whispered word was a name Eric had not expected to hear from Sparr.

"Oh, dear!" groaned a low voice.

A shape moved behind a wide marble column, and Eric raised his sword instinctively. "Who's there? Come out. Now!"

"Oh," came a second groan, as the familiar floppy-eared giant and caretaker of Zorfendorf's priceless library stepped into view.

"Do not hurt me —"

"Thog! Don't be afraid," said Eric, yanking his helmet off. "It's just me."

The shy-eyed giant searched Eric's face, blinked, and jumped. "It *is* you!" he said. "But your armor —"

"I'm in disguise," said Eric. "What are you still doing here? The gates have fallen."

"Words, words, words!" said Thog, gathering an armful of scrolls. "I must save them from the Ninns. There is never an end to the words." He reached past the perching birds.

"Even now, these silly creatures have brought more words! Look at this scrap of paper."

Eric took a small piece of parchment from the giant. A single line was penned on it.

His heart skipped as he read it.

Collect the magics.

"But that's exactly what I've been thinking!" he said. "The only real way to win this war is to . . ." He stopped. "Wait a second. I know this handwriting. These words were written by Quill, Galen's feather pen."

"Quill!" said Thog. "That clever little pen vanished from this library just days ago. The very same day as Galen . . ."

"Galen?" said Eric. "Do you think Galen is using Quill to tell us things? Do you think . . . Quill is actually *with* Galen?"

"They are the dearest of friends," said Thog. "Oh, the birds!"

Eric looked up in time to see a streak of feathers disappear through an upper window.

As if their work here was done!

Eric read the parchment again. If it really *was* from Galen, then his mission was clear. The quest he had imagined was the same as Galen's. It was set in three simple words.

Collect the magics.

He knew more than ever that *this* was what he had to do. And Sparr was his first goal.

"Surround the tower!" came a cry from inside the castle.

Thog shivered. "I must save what I can before the Ninns find this room. These scrolls are some of the castle's most prized possessions. Look. A map to the Seven Cities of Gold!"

Eric stared at the door Sparr had gone through. "I have to go. But . . . I've never heard of the Seven Cities of Gold. Where are they?"

Thog shrugged his massive shoulders. "The map is blank! But precious all the same. Prince Zorfendorf collected it long before I came here."

"I have to go," Eric repeated, remembering that the castle was named after the mysterious — and never seen — Prince Zorfendorf.

But the blank map intrigued him. On its corner he spied a silver stamp of a bare tree. The tiny emblem reminded him of the apple trees near his house, and of how his world was in as much danger as Droon.

The castle doors shuddered.

"I have to go!" Eric said for the third time. Stuffing Quill's mysterious message into his cloak, he whispered the name Sparr had uttered and entered a dim passage. He made his way down a flight of very dark stairs until an object swung down suddenly in front of his face.

Eric screamed. "Ahhh!"

The object screamed, too. "Ahhh!"

Jumping back, Eric flicked a spark from his fingertip and saw, dangling from the ceiling, a plump creature with orange hair.

It was Max the spider troll.

"Max! What are you doing here?"

The spider troll grinned. "When Gethwing flew you away, we had no choice. We all followed you!"

"We?" asked Eric.

"All of us," said Max. "Keeah, Neal, Julie. But we were separated in this battle. I'm all you have now." The spider troll paused. "Eric . . . it's happening, isn't it? The end of days?"

"No!" said Eric abruptly, even though the *end of days* was all he could think about. "I won't believe it. I refuse to believe it." He slipped his hand into his cloak and touched the Moon Medallion and the parchment next to it. *Collect the magics.* "Max, I'm on a quest to do what I can. Maybe it's my final quest, the biggest thing I've ever been called on to do, but Droon won't fall. I won't let it!"

Max tried to smile. "I will help you."

"Good." Eric placed his hands on the panel in front of him.

"Zara," he whispered for the second time. The panel slid aside. As always, his heart felt a pang of pain at the mention of her name.

"But why?" asked Max. "Why her name?"

Eric shook his head. "I don't know. I don't know anything. Look, you *can* help me. Take this." He withdrew the Moon Medallion from his cloak. "I've got to turn Sparr to our side. But if I can't, and he senses that I have this, he'll overpower me and steal it."

Max's face dropped as he took the powerful object. "I will protect it with my life."

"Let's hope it doesn't come to that," said Eric. "The moment I find out what he's up to, I'll want it back, so stay close, all right?"

"I'll be right here," said the spider troll.

Eric nodded once, then headed down the black staircase two steps at a time, smelling the damp of the earth behind the walls.

"Sparr?" he called. "Are you down here?"

The only answer was the sound of murmuring below.

The narrow stone stairs looked as ancient as Droon itself. But they were not.

The giant white castle of Zorfendorf was in fact only a few years old, conjured by Galen to hide the location of the legendary Fifth River, a magical waterway connecting Droon to the Upper World summoned long before by Zara herself. Using a spell as strong as his mother's original, Galen was later forced to bury the mystical river and seal forever the fountain through which it flowed.

Sparr can't be searching for the Fifth River . . . can he?

Stepping off the bottom stair, Eric sensed a thick, earthy aroma. He was far beneath the castle courtyard. Above him, he knew, stood the great white tower that Zorfendorf was famous for. It was in many ways like the tower over Jaffa City. Two cities. Two towers. Both under siege.

He listened. At first he heard only the beating of his heart. Then a quiet footfall, then another. He turned left toward a passage barely tall enough for him to walk upright and soon came to a solid wall of white stone.

The sorcerer emerged from the shadows. He was pale and trembling from head to foot.

"Sparr, what's wrong with you?"

"Never mind," said the sorcerer. "I have tried to open the door I know stands here, but I cannot. My mind is . . . Open this wall, Ungast. I know you know how. Do it!"

Good or evil, Sparr had a power over Eric that few possessed.

"Sure," he said. "But what are we —"

"Do it," Sparr repeated softly.

Eric nodded. Raising both hands to the wall, he searched his mind and was amazed to come up with the words — and amazed again when they tripped off his tongue like honey.

"*Selit-ka-fassa-noha. Zeetha-pa-koam!*"

"Ah, yes, yes," murmured the sorcerer.

Eric stood back as his words had their effect. The air rippled from ceiling to floor, and an arched entrance shimmered into view.

"And the quest continues," said Sparr.

"Quest?" Eric said. "What quest?"

Sparr moved ghostlike under the arch and stepped deliberately across the small chamber, his fingertips sparking. He paused once, twice, as if to listen, then moved on.

"What do you hear?" Eric asked.

Again, no answer. Sparr was leaden-faced, his eyes milky white, his arms rigid, as if in a world of his own. Yet Eric tried to reach him.

"Sparr, I need to talk to you. Really. It's about Gethwing. And his plans. For you."

Sparr walked silently around the pyramid of collapsed stone that was all that remained of his mother's magical fountain. Circling the stones, Sparr seemed unaware of the shouting of Ninns on the floors above.

Not knowing exactly what to say, but afraid that time was slipping away, Eric spoke.

"Lord Sparr, you need to know something . . . you call me Ungast, but . . . look, Droon will fall. And Gethwing's plans don't involve . . . all of us. He's got this prophecy, and I think we need to find out what it means. We can only do this by . . ."

He drew Quill's parchment from his cloak. "I don't know what you hope to find here, but I think Galen is trying to tell us —"

A blast thundered through the rooms above, followed by shouting and thudding footsteps. A moment later, the archway filled with a brigade of breathless Ninns.

"Lord Sparr!" one grunted. "The main rooms are taken. Shall we destroy the tower?"

"No!" cried Sparr, coming out of his trance for a moment. "No . . . no . . . I will deal with it myself. Leave us!"

"Yes, commander!" said the Ninns, climbing clumsily back up the stairs.

And Eric knew.

You are going to try to create the stone boat, aren't you? Your mother's boat? But what quest are you on? It can't be the same as mine . . . can it?

As Sparr gazed upon the rubble of the fountain, the three birds were suddenly there again, circling the ceiling. One was the color of rust, a second filthy white, and the third as black as oil. Eric watched their short, scuffling flight from stone to stone, his memory alive with birds he had seen long before.

"Shield your eyes," said the sorcerer. "The air now turns as silver as a new blade!"

Eric stepped back as the sorcerer raised his arms to the ceiling.

Moments later, the fountain's rubble jostled and quaked and shrieked.

And it began to move.

Three

The Living Stone

Sparr's fingertips flamed with black sparks as he urged the stones to come together. "Scene of sorrow, scene of loss, become a scene of triumph! Come, ship, come!"

Eric knew what had happened in that deep chamber. It *was* a sad scene, a scene of bitter loss, full of painful memories for Sparr.

The sorcerer's mother, Queen Zara, had built the fountain and the ship that grew out of its stones for one purpose only: to send her infant son to the Upper World, freeing him from Emperor Ko's ruthless rule.

But Ko tracked her down, and she collapsed before she could send her son into the freedom of his brother Urik's arms.

"Ship, I command you, *come*!" Sparr cried, urging the stones to take their magic shape.

But they would not.

"I must! They must!" he shouted. "She . . . she . . ."

As Eric watched, Sparr raged and coaxed. He chanted and shouted, he whispered and sang out, but the stones did no more than tremble in place.

"Fly, stones, fly!" he cried.

As Eric saw tears of anger rise in the sorcerer's eyes and felt his pain, he remembered his first time in the room and the single word that had caused the fountain to rise.

But Galen had uncharmed the fountain. He had buried the river. That word surely would not work anymore. Would it?

"O, tender face, face of sorrow, face of truth, mother, queen — take me to the Upper World," Sparr said. "My quest to find it must continue. I must bring it to you."

"What quest?" asked Eric. "To find what?"

Sparr swung around to him. "That which was lost, of course! Before *they* find it."

"But who? What are you talking about?"

Sparr narrowed his eyes at Eric. "Do you not see? This great world lies in tatters around us. Hours remain before Droon collapses, never to be seen again. It will happen soon unless I heed her command."

"What command?" Eric cried.

"To collect the magic that is lost!"

Eric staggered to hear those words again. "Collect the magic? From the Upper World? But what magic is *there*?"

"The castle is moments from falling," said the sorcerer. "Stones, fly! Fountain, appear!"

Eric's mind reeled. *If I help him, if I join my power to his, will Sparr join us again? Will*

he be the first of the magics? Is this my com-
mand, too?

As Eric set his feet firmly apart, he knew he had answered his own questions. Secretly directing his fingers at the base of the crumbled fountain, he silently spoke the word he knew, the word set there by Sparr's mother.

Ythra!

At once, the stones obeyed. They began to swivel and roll across one another, round and round, thudding one after another into place.

Unaware of Eric's involvement, Sparr laughed. "Look! I am doing it! Ungast, tremble before my awesome power!"

"I'm trembling, all right," said Eric, using all his might to move the giant stones.

"Now, watch this!" said Sparr.

Eric mimicked every twist of the sorcerer's hand to urge the frozen stones to join.

And they did.

The stones hung together in the air as if suspended by the power of Sparr's magic alone.

Stone by stone, Zara's fountain grew, while Eric strained his powers to their limit.

Helping Sparr reminded him of the day he and his father had installed the swing set in his backyard. Sparr's expression was full of glee, just as his father's had been when they worked side by side.

Foom! Foom! The stones collided and hung together as if meant to be joined, never to be parted. Rock on rock, stone on stone, Zara's mysterious creation rose before their eyes.

"Look how I reverse the old one's magic with my own!" said Sparr.

Not your own, thought Eric, but he knew who Sparr meant. "Sparr, I think Galen is . . . I think he's trying to communicate with me . . . with us . . . ."

"Yes, yes," said Sparr, "as you say. But look, the Fifth River comes! I know it —"

Sparr was right, for the floor beneath their feet had already begun to quake and the roar of water to fill the stony chamber.

"And more!" cried Sparr. "Fly, stones, fly!"

Then, with the thunderous roar of stone impacting stone, the fountain began to change itself into a ship.

A ship of stone.

The levels, the spouts, the rims, the angles, the pediment itself grew into decks and railings and masts. A prow emerged, needle sharp. Ghostly rigging, like cobwebs of iron, stretched from the top of massive masts to the deck railings below.

Great red sails, like the wings of an enormous jungle bird, billowed out, poised and waiting for flight. The scrollwork etched in the stone that made up the hull, the coiled railings, the tapered mast itself — all were crude and delicate at the same time.

All the while, the water beneath the castle thundered and roared, until the sorcerer stiffened. "The figurehead!" He breathed in mightily and made as if to pick up a massive stone.

Oh, not that one! thought Eric, trying to

keep up. Using all his strength, he sent a beam of invisible energy across the chamber.

The heavy stone looked as if it weighed a thousand pounds, but Sparr "lifted" it as if it were no more than a pillow. Eric gasped in pain to keep so many things going at once.

"See there?" said Sparr.

"Right," groaned Eric, barely able to stand.

Then he *did* see something.

A narrow ridge on the surface of the stone encircled a head like a crown. Before Eric could stop himself, he spoke the name.

"Zara!"

Sparr flew around and stared at Eric. "You see her?" he asked. "She speaks to you, too?"

But when Eric looked back at the stone, the image of Zara's face, if that was what it was, had vanished. It was rough stone once more.

"How about we put it down now?" asked Eric.

"It's as light as a feather!" said Sparr, showing no signs of fatigue. "And we finish!"

Sparr "hurled" the stone to the bow of the ship and — *FOOOOM!* — the vessel was complete.

Though the water continued to rush beneath the floor, silence seemed to follow the last tumultuous joining of stones.

Sparr relaxed. "It barely took anything out of me," he said. "I must be getting stronger!"

"Oh, I'm sure," said Eric, rubbing his arms.

"So. We are ready," said the sorcerer. "Let us board, you and me."

Not without the Medallion, thought Eric. "Okay, but first I need something," he said hastily. "Some . . . supplies!"

Sparr turned. "Supplies? What supplies?"

"Stuff. Bows, arrows, food. You know. Stuff!"

"Be quick about it!" said Sparr. "We are in the presence of great power — mine!"

Eric scurried under the arch to the passage outside. *Max,* he said silently, *if you can hear me, I need you now. Bring me the Medallion!*

Slowly Sparr mounted the plank.

As the battle reached a crescendo in the passages above, a stone in the wall next to Eric squeaked aside. Max's orange hair was just visible in the darkness. He handed the silver Medallion through, and Eric slipped it inside his cloak.

"I heard you ask for supplies," whispered Max with a wink. "I found something better."

The spider troll grunted as he pushed a large chest into the hallway. "Whew!"

"I wasn't thinking of anything this big," groaned Eric, trying to lift the chest.

"Are you done out there?" asked Sparr.

"Nearly," Eric called back. "Max, what do you have in this trunk?"

"You mean *who!*" said a muffled voice.

The chest lid cracked open and a pair of eyes peeped out. Eric blinked. "Keeah?"

"You asked for reinforcements, didn't you?" the princess of Droon whispered.

"We're all here," said Julie. She was crouching inside the chest, next to Neal.

Eric wanted to hug them all. "You guys! I can't believe you're all here! We need to get on board. Sparr is heading for the Upper World on a quest for something magical. We need it. And him. But he's a little out of it, so hide until you hear from me."

"Or until we *don't* hear from you," said Neal.

"What's taking so long?" called Sparr.

"Coming!" Eric said. "Sorry about this, guys —"

"Sorry about what?" asked Keeah.

Eric pushed Max into the chest, slammed down the lid, dragged the heavy box to the ship, and heaved it onto the deck with a *thump*.

"Finally!" said Sparr. "And now we fly!"

Spreading his arms wide, the sorcerer chanted over and over. Eric knew what was wanted, so he murmured a charm, and the ceiling of the chamber peeled away to reveal the inside of the white tower.

Eric's heart turned to ice.

At the very top was a sky darkening with smoke. Flames edged over the lip of the tower.

The final war. Burning. Ashes!

"Ungast, take the wheel!" Sparr cried.

As Eric clambered to the upper deck, a brigade of Ninns swarmed into the room.

"Lord Sparr!" they shouted.

"Ungast!" Sparr cried.

His ears still ringing with Gethwing's dire words, Eric grasped the stone wheel in both hands and turned it. The ship lurched up, crashed out of the chamber, and surged skyward through the inside of the white tower.

"Lord Sparr!" called the Ninns.

The red-faced warriors stared at their departing leader, whose eyes focused only on the skies above. Eric saw astonishment and awe in their faces, but also sorrow.

He knew what they felt. Sparr was always leaving them behind.

"To the Upper World!" bellowed Sparr.

With that, the ship made of stone rose on the torrent of water, straight up the great white tower and into the sky.

Four

Revenge of the Hunters

Water gushed around the ship and propelled it through the hollow tower with such force that Eric was thrown onto his back.

"Sparr! Hey, Sparr!"

But from his place at the bow the sorcerer only laughed and bellowed like a child on a carnival ride. "Up we go! Up we go!"

The chest Julie, Neal, Keeah, and Max were hiding in slid the entire length of the deck until it wedged against the main mast.

"Tie it down or lose it!" said Sparr, still laughing.

Eric chained the chest to the mast. "Tie it down? I'm getting inside!" He whipped open the wooden chest, leaped in, and closed the lid over him. Then he gasped in surprise.

The inside of the chest was not two feet by three feet as he expected, but much larger. It was, in fact, the size of a huge room.

And it was furnished!

Carpets were laid across the floor, stools were gathered around a low table, the ceiling was draped in fabric like a desert outpost, and flaming lanterns hung from wrought-iron hooks on the walls.

"No wonder it was so heavy," he groaned.

"Eric!" said Keeah, whipping him around with a great smile. "We couldn't simply abandon you on the quest. Now it's just like old times!"

The chest rattled and shook.

"Old dangerous times," said Neal. "I feel like we're being shot out of a fire hose!"

"Only faster," said Eric. "Sparr is piloting this thing into our world. He's after something he thinks Zara is telling him to find. But he's kind of in a trance."

The shaking suddenly lessened.

"We're slowing down," said Keeah.

Together, the kids and Max popped open the lid of the chest and looked out. As in Droon, it was night, but by the light of the rising moon they saw a body of calm water spread out around them. Directly ahead, under the glare of several spotlights, stood a wall of dark stone twenty feet high.

"This doesn't look familiar," Neal whispered. "Where are we?"

"Is that the wall of a fortress?" Keeah asked. "Are we still in Droon?"

With a stroke of his hand, Sparr dashed the rigging, bringing the ship to a standstill. "I fear this is not the Upper World . . ."

"Yes, it is," Julie whispered, peering around.

"This is the hydroelectric dam at Silver Lake. Our class visited here on a field trip. It's about ten miles upriver from" — she pointed behind them — "our town."

Eric clambered out of the chest and onto the upper deck. He saw his town downhill from the dam, its street and house lights twinkling.

"I remember that class trip," he said.

"I don't," said Neal.

"You were there with us," said Julie.

"Oh, I'm sure I was there," said Neal. "All I remember are the ham sandwiches."

"What ham sandwiches?" Julie asked.

"The ones the bus driver shared only with me," said Neal with a smile.

The ship drifted to the middle of the lake, and Sparr turned toward Eric.

"Better hide for now," Eric whispered, and Max clamped the lid of the chest closed.

But Sparr swiveled suddenly and leaned over the deck railing. As he stared into the water, his entire frame froze, his eyes glazed over, and he began murmuring to himself again. "Zara . . . tell me where . . ."

"Sparr, if I knew what you were looking for —" said Eric.

All at once, something whizzed past his head, spitting black sparks at him. They crackled against his armor, knocking him down. The thing soared up and dived again.

"Steer the ship into the inlet!" said Eric, scrambling to his feet. "Sparr —"

But the sorcerer kept staring into the lake as if possessed, whispering softly.

Eric kicked open the chest. "Sparr's in dreamland, guys. Help me!"

The object swooped down again, and the friends flattened to the deck as another spray of black sparks sizzled at them.

"What is that thing?" Julie asked.

"Who's attacking us?" Neal said.

"There!" said Keeah. "Look! It's them!"

A shadow moved quickly across the very top of the concrete dam. At first, Eric thought it was a trick of the spotlights. But it was soon followed by a second figure, and a third.

"Holy cow!" said Neal. "I'd know those creepy shapes anywhere."

"It's the Hunters," said Julie, "and their nasty spark ball! What do they want here?"

"Perhaps the same thing Sparr does?" said Max. "Something magical?"

The same thing I'm looking for? Eric wondered.

The sorcerer leaned even closer to the water, rolling his head from side to side.

"No matter why they're here," said Neal, "that spiky baseball is coming again!"

They ducked as the ball swung low, bounced across the deck, and crashed into the mast before taking flight again.

"Retreat!" called Max. "Catch the wind to the inlet before we lose Zara's ship!"

Keeah, Julie, and Neal unfurled the sails, and Eric spun the wheel sharply. The breeze across the lake filled the red sails, and they were soon out of range of the Hunters' ball.

"Gethwing sent them to our world for a reason," Keeah said. "Maybe now we'll find out what that is."

Neal pulled a tiny telescope from his turban. "I see they still have their toys with them," he said.

While one of the Hunters wielded the spark-spitting ball, another carried a short dagger with a wavy blade, and the third sported a pair of magical silver boots that made him as swift as the wind.

"The last time we saw them," said Julie, "the Hinkles were following them. Maybe they couldn't find them —"

"Spoke too soon," said Max. "Eric, I think I see your parents!"

And there they were.

Mr. and Mrs. Hinkle scurried across the top of the dam wall. Before the kids could warn them, the Hunters jumped out of hiding and lunged at the two grown-ups.

"I don't think so!" said Neal. "We need to rescue your folks, Eric —"

"On it!" Eric shot a beam of silver sparks straight up the wall of the dam. It flared in front of the Hunters and sent them leaping away from his parents. Keeah followed with a spray of violet sparks, and the evil trio raced back across the wall to a three-story brick structure at the far end of the dam.

Leaving the ship anchored in the inlet, the children ran to the shore toward the Hinkles. Eric got there first and surprised his father, who waved a hefty stick at him.

"Stop right there, or face my wrath, you purple bad guy!" Mr. Hinkle said.

"Ditto!" cried Mrs. Hinkle, waving a stick of her own.

"Mom, Dad, it's me," Eric said. His heart racing, he removed his helmet and stepped toward them. "It's just me . . ."

Mrs. Hinkle burst into tears. She tossed her stick down and wrapped her arms around her son. "Eric! We've been so worried . . ."

"Eric, are you all right?" his father asked.

"Yes," Eric said. "And no. Look, Droon will fall" — he gauged the position of the moon — "in twenty-seven hours, unless we stop Gethwing."

"The sun dragon," said Mr. Hinkle, nodding.

"The moon dragon," Eric said. "Lord Sparr is here to find something magic. I think it's the same thing the Hunters want to bring to Gethwing. We're all looking for the same thing."

"We'd better get back to the ship," said Keeah. "This way."

They wound their way back to the ship and paused when they saw Sparr standing on the deck like a statue of black marble.

"I'm not sure I like the look of that guy," said Mr. Hinkle. "Can we trust him?"

"We have to," said Eric.

Mrs. Hinkle shook her head. "Evil guys and their outfits. After this, Eric, I want you to run home and put on some regular clothes. You really don't look good in purple."

"Or armor," said his father.

"I know," he said. "But I'm not done with this disguise just yet. There's work to do."

"Here, too," said his mother, scanning the nearby woods. "Your father and I tracked those sneaky Hunters to this lake. It's bad enough they're here at all, but we really got mad when they kidnapped your friend."

Neal frowned. "Our friend? Who?"

"You know her," said Mr. Hinkle. "She used to go to your school. You know, the girl with the long dark hair."

"Went to our —" Julie started.

"Meredith!" the children gasped together.

"Meredith is my aunt!" said Keeah.

"No, honestly, she was in their homeroom," said Eric's mother.

"No, honestly," Max said, "she's Keeah's aunt. In human form. Otherwise known as Witch Demither."

Meredith had been a student at the kids' school. It was only when Gethwing attacked their town that they'd learned the girl was actually Witch Demither, who had been charmed into a regular girl with a mission in the Upper World.

"That's the power plant," Mr. Hinkle said, pointing to the squat brick building at the end of the dam. "Those nasty guys have set up headquarters there. Witch Meredith is inside."

Keeah turned to the ship. "They're all here for the same thing. The Hunters, Sparr, and Demither. We need to free her. Follow me —"

"Alas, Urik!" Sparr shouted suddenly. "I do not see it! It cannot be done!"

"Urik?" Eric turned to the ship. "But —"

Max held him back. "I will see to Sparr. You save Demither. Go."

Eric ran along with the others, but he wondered what possible connection the lake could have with Urik. Had Zara sent Sparr for something belonging to Urik?

The more he thought about it, the more he remembered something Meredith had once told him.

She'd said that water flowed everywhere and joined everything, all places in all worlds.

"Everything is connected," she had said. "Past, present, future, place to other place, everything. All things connect."

To prove it, she had written her name on the surface of the swimming pool at his school. He could never forget the stunning moment when she rearranged the letters.

Meredith

became

Demither

It proved yet again how names and words were some of the greatest magic of all.

Carefully, the children crept toward the dam. They were no more than fifty yards away when the spiked ball flew out of the brick building.

"Duck!" said Neal.

Only the ball wasn't aimed at them. It soared high, sizzling with energy, then dived straight down at the dam wall. It struck with tremendous speed and exploded, sending chunks of cement and stone into the air.

Before the children knew what was happening, the middle of the dam had collapsed. The calm lake water heaved once, twice, three times, then rushed over the broken wall.

"No! No!" cried Eric as thousands of gallons of water hurtled toward the helpless town below.

Five

Underwater, Underground

Water gushed through the cracked wall and plummeted down the side of the dam. The hillside flooded. Trees crashed to the ground, their roots clawing upward. More and more of the lake rushed through the gap, and the entire dam began to cave in.

Within moments, the water became an unstoppable force, a monstrous tidal wave, rolling toward the town.

Mrs. Hinkle fell to her knees. "Our friends!"

"Thousands of innocent people!" cried Mr. Hinkle. "We have to do something!"

Eric turned to his friends. "Keeah, you and me —"

"I know," she said. "We have to do this together. I only hope we can!"

"We need more than hope," said Eric.

As larger and larger portions of the dam fell into the rushing water, the two wizards scrambled to the top of the wall.

"Like old times, Eric!" Keeah said.

Her violet sparks met and entwined with his silver ones. Together, they blasted at the water, managing to ensnare it with pure energy, holding it up behind a wall of light.

The waves churned on the near side of their magic wall, growing higher and stronger.

Neal searched his genie scroll for a charm to conjure the concrete back into place. He managed to send one giant block flying back up, but it did little good. The water simply flowed higher and higher behind Eric and Keeah's wall of light.

"I can't put the dam back together!" Neal shouted. "We need more magic!"

More magic! thought Eric. *More than we have!*

From across the lake came Sparr's cry, "I have found it! I have found it!"

Keeah's sparks were being split apart, sizzling and fizzling. "I . . . can't . . . it's not holding —"

"Sparr!" cried Eric. **Sparr, help us! We need you —**

Instantly, Sparr broke out of his trance.

"Why didn't you say so!" He whipped his cloak behind him and flew to Eric and Keeah. "Repair the wall! I'll take on the water —"

As if once more his powerful self, Lord Sparr climbed to the top of the wall and raced along it, jumping over the torrent of rushing water. Then, like an arrow, he leaped from the summit and disappeared.

"Keeah, come with me," called Eric. "Julie, Neal, fly my parents to safety!"

"We're already on it," said Neal.

Letting the water go, Keeah and Eric worked together to hurl massive chunks of concrete back into place. Max was there now, too. He speedily wove a web as strong as iron and spun it around the broken concrete to keep the loose chunks fast.

"I hope Sparr can do it!" said Keeah.

"Sparr, here!" yelled Eric. And he sent the Moon Medallion flying to the sorcerer, who grasped it and hung it around his neck.

Taking up a position on a high rock, Sparr stood fast. The veins on his neck grew taut. The jagged scar on his forehead turned bright red, as if it had been made afresh. His eyes, huge and black, focused on the giant waves as they grew higher and higher.

Then, as if the Medallion flared and a flame entered him, Sparr let out a fierce yell.

"Back, back, ye waters, into thy place!"

And the water, as if it were a living creature, coiled itself into a roaring tower. It rose and rose, snaking into the air high over the dam. It arched over Sparr's head and seemed to snarl and gasp at him. But the Medallion flared once more, and the water fell back up the hill. Every last drop hurled itself over the dam wall into the emptying lake bed.

Waving his hands once, Sparr calmed the waters, and the lake became as peaceful as it had been before the dam burst.

Sparr kept his hands poised over the water for a minute, two minutes, his face twisted from the exertion, until finally he breathed out and collapsed to the ground.

Everyone ran to him. After a moment or two, they managed to revive him.

"I take back what I said," said Mr. Hinkle. "I kind of like this guy!"

"Thank you," Sparr whispered.

Then he shook his head from side to side and bolted to his feet, a new man. "Eric, take the Medallion. I am myself. Demither is part of why I am here. Come! Follow! Save her! Our quest continues!"

Without a word, the friends raced after him to the brick building at the end of the dam.

They crept carefully up to its dirt-stained windows and looked in. The giant room inside was dimly lit, but they could see huge pistons thumping while great wheels turned and rods and gears ground incessantly.

"She's in there," said Keeah. "I sense her."

"We must free the Sea Witch," said Sparr. "I see now that we need Demither. Without her, this quest may not succeed."

"Let me see what I can find out." Julie stepped back from the group and leaped into the air. She circled the top of the squat building and then returned. "There's a ladder to the roof on the far side and an entrance into the plant from up there. The Hunters won't expect us to surprise them that way."

Neal grinned. "Cool. The element of surprise. It'll be like Christmas morning for the Hunters. Only *we'll* be the presents and it won't be as much fun . . . for them."

Sparr's eyes twinkled. "Let's do it."

Together the band of friends climbed up the ladder and hopped over a low wall onto the roof. They could feel the ceaseless throb of machinery beneath their feet.

Neal darted straight to a raised brick shed. "A locked door?" he said. "Not so much."

Adjusting his turban, he flicked his fingers, and the lock clicked open. While the Hinkles kept guard on the roof, Sparr, the children, and Max crept one by one down a set of metal stairs to a catwalk overlooking an immense power generator.

"There she is," whispered Max.

Meredith's long, dark hair was tangled and wet, but her young face was calm as she glared at the three gangly Hunters. Her hands were bound behind her to a fat steel girder.

"Her chains must be preventing her from becoming a serpent," whispered Keeah. "Otherwise she'd turn the tables on those Hunters."

"And the chairs and dishes and place mats and everything," said Neal.

Sparr pressed a finger to his lips. "Listen closely. They are questioning her."

"Where?" the first Hunter hissed.

"Where?" said the second.

"Where?" said the third.

Meredith followed each one with her eyes. Then she said, "Uh, can you repeat the question?"

Keeah smiled. "That's Aunt Demither."

Sparr nodded. "Neal, take out the lights. Julie, fly quietly down behind the Hunters and prepare to leap. Keeah and Max, create a diversion. Eric, you and I will release Demither. These fiends cannot remain in your world. They must return with us. Ready?"

They all nodded.

Sparr grinned. "And . . . go!"

When Julie leaped up, Neal charmed the lights to flare out. At the same time, Max swung quietly down behind Meredith, and Keeah shot a single violet spark across the large room. It struck an iron wheel, ricocheted, and hit a steel drum.

All three Hunters jerked around at once.

"Now!" said Sparr.

The friends leaped into action. It went like clockwork. The surprised Hunters scrambled in every direction at once. Julie flew from one to the other, tripping them. Keeah forced them down, and Max bound them in strong spider silk.

Twin streams of sparks from Eric and Sparr quickly dissolved the chains on Meredith. The action was over before she even jumped to her feet.

Keeah bowed before her aunt. "Meredith. Demither!"

"Thank you all," she said. "I'm Meredith for now. We have loads of work to do. But first . . ."

She turned to Sparr. "You cursed me."

Sparr lowered his head. "I did. I will not lie. You were a threat to me. The *world* was a threat to me. But now . . . I am changed."

"And why should I believe you?" she asked.

"There is no excuse for what I did," Sparr said. "And I shall pay for it. But look in your heart. A greater cause demands we work together."

Keeah took her aunt aside. "It's true. Even as we speak, Gethwing marches on Jaffa City with the largest army of beasts ever assembled. My father and my mother — your sister — bravely defend a falling city, hoping against hope that the tide will turn. But the beasts are legion. Hundreds of thousands of them march over the land. Millions. They are unstoppable."

Meredith was silent for a long moment before her face changed. "Very well. I can help. I *will* help. Perhaps we *are* in this together. Dreams day and night pursued me until a spell of such power took me away from Droon and led me here. There was a reason. Gethwing sent the Hunters after me to trap me and force me to find something for him. I didn't know myself what it was. I wandered your world, trying to discover what I searched for. Always I returned to this lake."

"As I do now," said Sparr. "It lies under the

waves. I know it. But alone, I have not the magic to retrieve it. I need more. I need you."

"Then . . . let's find it," Meredith said.

"But what exactly are you talking about?" Keeah asked. "Meredith?"

Saying nothing, the girl made her way outside the building, where Eric's parents were waiting. They all followed her to the lakeshore where, with barely a sound, she slipped beneath its surface and breathed the water as if it were air.

When she came up, her hair was a tangle of strands that coiled like eels. Her skin, dark green and glistening, was formed of scales, and her eyes were as red as flame. Beneath the surface, her body twisted away into a long, finned tail.

Mrs. Hinkle gasped. "Oh, my!"

"You see me in my true form," she said. Then she pointed to the center of the lake, which was black in the shadow of the pine trees. "It lies down there."

"It does?" said Neal. "Wait. What does?"

"Like Demither, my travels led me all over the Upper World," Sparr said. "You children know this. My brother Urik followed me through time. It was during this journey through time that I first experienced the tangle that is our past and our future."

The Sea Witch nodded. "How it loops upon itself. How an object, even a powerful one, can be trapped in time's twists and turns."

"I had it for a while," said Sparr. "Galen certainly did. Eric, you had it."

"I did?" he said.

"Yet time swept it away," Demither said. "Over and over it was found, lost, found, lost."

"Until now," said the sorcerer.

Their conversation was like a strange duet of storytellers, each adding another part of the tale. Eric tried to understand what Demither and Sparr were talking about, when Julie suddenly gasped. "Are you talking about the Wand of Urik?"

Sparr smiled. "Just so. Let us retrieve it, for the sands of time fall rapidly. To the ship!"

"That leaves us out," said Mr. Hinkle. "I'm not a lake person. We'll wait on shore."

His head buzzing with questions, Eric helped his friends haul the Hunters to the ship. They sailed it to the center of the lake.

The Wand of Urik! he thought. *Of course! It was one of the most magical of objects in both worlds. But like its maker, it was lost in time!*

"Hold on," Neal said. "This really is the deepest part of the whole lake. Don't tell us we have to . . ."

"I *am* telling you!" said Demither.

With a twist of her hands, she conjured a helmet of air for each of them. "Now dive!"

They did dive, deep under the surface to the very bottom of the lake where the water was as black as oil. Sparr and Demither swam on as if they could see in the dark.

When they stopped, there it was, hazy at first, then growing in detail until they could all plainly see it . . . a sequence of images moving like a film.

Eric's heart skipped as he saw a boy, young Galen, holding the magic wand he knew so well. At its tip blossomed a vibrant purple flower whose petals were part of its magic.

"The Wand of Urik!" Lord Sparr declared. "It lies trapped in a loop of time."

It did seem like that, as the story of the wand replayed itself in front of them.

At first it was in Galen's hand. Then it was stolen by a goblin. It reappeared in Ko's hand. Then Eric's, then Sparr's, then Galen's again.

It dawned on Eric exactly what he was seeing. It was as if the world — as if both worlds, the Upper one and Droon — combined in a single place and time.

"When he was young, Galen used Urik's wand to create the rainbow stairs," Eric said. "After that, he lost it in Droon to a goblin, who brought it to Ko. I found it at Ko's tomb and brought it to the Upper World when I followed Sparr up the Dark Stair into the past. That was when Galen was given the wand.

He used it for the staircase, then the wand was lost and found again and lost again."

"It really is a time tangle," said Julie.

"And here comes my headache," Neal said.

"One of us alone could not have found the wand," said the Sea Witch. "Nor can one of us alone retrieve it."

"It is my mother's vision of us," said Sparr. "Working together."

"To collect the magics," Eric said out loud for the first time. "It's Galen's vision, too."

Demither turned to him and smiled. "All things connect."

Sparr made his way closer to the moving images, but they resisted his approach, fading away and reappearing only when he stepped away.

Demither tried the same, reaching out as the wand passed from one person to the next. Each time she moved, the scene changed.

"Time!" said Neal. "It's enough to drive you crazy."

"Maybe we can't retrieve the wand," Max said. "Maybe it really is lost in time forever."

Eric watched closely and glimpsed a moment, a single instant, when the wand appeared to touch the ground with no one's hand upon it. He moved toward young Galen and watched the sequence of images play again and again. Finally, he seemed to catch the young wizard's eye.

Galen's hand loosened.

The wand fell to the ground.

Or it *would* have fallen to the ground if Eric had not grasped it in his fingers an instant before it struck.

When he drew his hand away, he was holding the Wand of Urik. "I have it!" he cried.

In a flash, the friends surfaced and climbed aboard the stone ship once more.

"Holy cow, Eric, you did it!" gasped Neal, yanking off his air helmet. "That was so cool!"

"I did it," Eric said, still stunned that he had found a way where others had not.

Collect the magics? I'm doing it!

The wand's power screamed through Eric's veins. The heat of it shocked him. "Sparr, take it. Please."

The moment the sorcerer wrapped his fingers around the wand, its tip blossomed with new sharp petals, as purple as the ocean at night, and Sparr underwent a change.

All at once, he was Young Sparr again. Then he was the ancient sorcerer Eric had seen in the Underworld, then the teenage Sparr whom they had battled in the desert long ago.

Even Shadowface, the evil side of the sorcerer, appeared, before dissolving away to leave only the Sparr the children had met so long ago on their first day in Droon.

"My journey enters a new phase," Sparr said with a smile. "I've come full circle and then some. A new chapter begins. I'm back!"

"Speaking of back," said Max. "We should be getting —"

All at once, the lake bubbled and splashed.

"Not again!" said Julie. "Everyone on your guard!"

A narrow metal tower rose out of the heaving waves. It was followed by a complex construction of decks, smokestacks, ladders, cables, fins, tentacles, propellers, hatches, railings, and keels.

"My goodness!" Max chirped. "If I didn't know better, I would say that that was one of Galen's earliest underwater motor devices!"

The strange vessel chugged toward them and stopped. A large round hatch swung open, and the wide red face of a Ninn popped out. He looked all around, saw the friends in the stone boat, and grinned. "Halloooo!"

"Captain Bludge?" said Sparr.

"At your service, my lord!" Bludge chirped.

The children had met Thumpinius Bludge several times before. The last time was in the red deserts of Koomba, from where Bludge and his Ninns had set off to find Sparr.

"How did you ever get here?" asked Keeah.

"We went searching for you, Lord Sparr," said the Ninn captain. "Alas, we drove off course. But we found you anyway! The truth is, our pilot said he knew the way."

"Which has nothing at all to do with me!" said a voice from below. "You're welcome!"

Bludge grumbled. "Meet our pilot."

Out popped the old face and long white beard of Nelag. He looked at the starry sky and frowned. "Good morning!"

Nelag was an *un*wizard. He was Galen's negative self and was known for saying and doing the opposite of what was considered normal.

"I said, 'Fly to the desert!'" Nelag said with a yawn. "That's why we sailed here."

Two other faces now peeped out of the submarine. Both faces belonged to Kem, the two-headed dog.

"Kem!" said the sorcerer. "My puppy!"

"Rooooo!" Sparr's two-headed pet dog yelped when he saw his master. He leaped from the sub straight onto the deck of the stone ship. Sparr swept his childhood friend into his arms.

"In case anyone wants to know," Nelag said, "I have *not* had any dream from Zara. She does *not* want you to bring her the wand. And especially not *immediately*!"

The children looked at one another.

Neal blinked. "Holy cow, our quest . . ."

"Continues!" said Julie.

"We have the wand," said Eric. "And Sparr. And the Moon Medallion. And Demither."

"We are collecting the magics!" said Keeah.

"Then raise the rigging!" boomed Sparr. "Unfurl the sail! Our quest continues!"

"Don't follow us back to Droon!" said Nelag, standing suddenly on his hands. "We don't know the way!"

"To Bangledorn Forest," shouted Keeah. "And the tomb of the Lost Queen!"

Six

The Falling City

Sparr stood at the wheel of the stone ship, Kem at his side. "The time is now. Demither, if you please . . ."

"The worlds connect through water," she said. "That's my department. Here goes!"

Demither underwent a second change. Her green tail darkened beneath the water and grew. Her features vanished into the frightening visage of a serpent — horned, finned, and giant — though her eyes remained fiery and glistening. She was now an enormous sea creature. "Prepare the ships! We travel!"

"Hinkles, board the stone ship for the journey of a lifetime!" called Max, and the ship swung to shore and the plank was lowered.

Mr. Hinkle stepped back, tugging Mrs. Hinkle with him. "I have an idea that your mother and I might be in the way."

"There's plenty of room, Dad," said Eric. "It's a magic ship."

"Oh, I'm sure it is, but . . ."

Mrs. Hinkle smiled. "What your father is trying to say, dear, is that you'll probably do better without us. Sailing between worlds in a magical stone boat is for the young at heart."

Knowing that the next few hours would be the most dangerous of his life, Eric went down the plank to them. "Thanks, Mom and Dad. You really helped today. But . . ."

"We know," said his father, tapping his knuckles on Eric's purple armor. "There's more to do. Stay safe. Really."

"I'll do my best," said Eric.

"Tell our parents we're all right," said Julie.

"We will," said Mrs. Hinkle.

"Good luck with mine," said Neal. "My folks worry about me getting on the bus every morning. And off the bus. And getting into school. To my desk. To lunch . . ."

"It means they love you," said Mrs. Hinkle.

Neal breathed deeply. "Yeah. Ditto. If things happen as they should, we'll be home soon."

Eric hugged his parents one last time before he mounted the plank to the deck once more.

But Neal's word — *soon* — flickered in his mind. Gethwing had used it, too. So had Sparr. And though he and his friends had begun to collect magical objects, he was sure the final element of Gethwing's prophecy predicted Droon's fall into ashes, and he was afraid his beloved Droon would be no more.

Soon? We'll be home soon?

Sure. And maybe never leave home again.

Demither swam around the perimeter of the lake in a wide circle. With each lap, she went faster around the stone ship and the antique submarine until a whirling wall of water grew high around them.

Clinging to his friends as the ship spun, Eric remembered the day Droon began for them. "What did we ever do before we found Droon?" he whispered.

Julie's face went pale. "I . . . can't remember. It's . . . everything."

"With all of you there," Keeah said.

"Let's not even think about it," said Neal. "A world without Droon is . . ."

He drifted off, unable to find the word.

"Exactly," said Eric. He recalled how the Droon adventure really started when his mother gave him a handful of garbage bags and told him to clean out the basement.

Garbage bags!

That simple chore had changed his life, for in the basement that day he, Julie, and Neal had discovered the rainbow staircase.

And then? Well, that was a long story.

A long story that might be in its final hours.

"Tighten the rigging!" shouted Max. "Be lively there. Rapids ahead!"

The Hunters, bound hand and foot, hissed and spat and cried to be released, but Max snatched their magical tools away, tightened their bonds, and dumped them into Keeah's magical trunk, which only made them cry louder.

All at once, the Ninns' submarine vanished into the depths of the whirling lake. Next went Demither herself, her finned tail coiling high. Finally, the storm of water rose over the stone ship's mast, and it, too, plummeted below the surface.

"Down the drain!" cried Neal. "Blub-blub!"

While Neal, Julie, and Max clung to the railing, Eric linked arms with Keeah, but whether to keep her safe or to steady himself, he was not sure.

As Demither had said, all water connects, and soon they were riding the waves of the Fifth River. It coiled upon itself and pushed the stone ship — like thread through the eye of a needle — into a tunnel of darkness so thick they couldn't tell whether they were sailing forward or backward or up or down.

A moment later, however, they were shot out into the air. But not from the magical fountain at Zorfendorf. The ship skidded to a stop in the main courtyard of Jaffa City!

The city was a storm of chaos.

The beast armies were on the attack. A wave of armored groggles had just broken through the gates with an enormous dragon-headed battering ram.

"Semirakin!" Sparr called out, and his faithful winged pilka appeared out of the twisting ribbons of smoke. Leaping to its back, he whistled.

"Rooo!" Kem howled, and he jumped into the saddle with his master.

"Time flies, and so must I," said Sparr, Urik's blossoming wand sizzling in his hand. "The quest continues. Meet us in the forests of Bangledorn!"

Flame glinted on his fins as a barrage of fire-tipped spears shot past him. Ignoring the danger, the black pilka took wing over the eastern wall.

Even before Kem's parting howl faded, a terrifying *thwang* screamed across the air.

"Shields up!" shouted King Zello, charging across the courtyard with a band of guards as a wall of fleet-flying arrows struck metal and wood with a stomach-churning *thunk*.

"We'll take the Hunters!" Zello growled. "Children, into the palace with you —"

"Father!" cried Keeah, rushing to him.

Viper-headed warriors in chariots burst into the square and shot across the cobblestones. "The princess! Take her!" they cried.

But with a wide swing of his arm, King Zello swept Keeah out of the way. Following up with his club, he swung hard from behind. The chariots' wheels shrieked and swerved sharply, toppling their snaky passengers.

"Daughter," Zello said breathlessly, "your

mission is great, but it is not here. Follow your mother. She has found a way out —"

A caped figure raced between the enemy lines toward them. It was Queen Relna. "Keeah, friends, follow me. The red wolves will guide you from the city."

"Sister, I will stay," said Demither to Queen Relna. "Let me help you."

"I won't, either," said Nelag, scrambling out of the dented submarine.

"The seawall," said Relna. "We are most defenseless there. You can both help."

"I shall try not to," Nelag said as he and Witch Demither hurried toward the seawall.

"See you later!" Neal called out to them.

"Yes, you won't!" said the fake wizard.

Eric's heart skipped a beat. *You won't . . .*

"My little band will infiltrate the Ninn armies," said Captain Bludge. "Who knows? Maybe by the end of the day you'll see a mess of Orkins at your royal table!"

"The wolves await," said Relna. "Come."

The friends entered the castle and plunged into the tunnels that ran beneath the city.

The underground streets, like the remains of an age-old civilization, were dark, narrow, and unused. Cobwebs hung from the ceiling across every intersection like a warning of dangers to come.

When Eric brushed them away with his sword — Ungast's sword — he remembered once more that his quest to collect the magics would end with Gethwing himself.

Neal's vision revealed Eric in the Cave of Night at the end. Gethwing had promised it, too. And it would be cold there. *Far colder than here*, the dragon had said. *But where was it?*

Eric's heart was sick with fear and sadness. But he could do little now but keep running.

A few moments later, Relna paused. The place was dark. In that moment of quiet, they heard the regular squealing of stones, as of some distant door opening, closing, opening again. It sounded like the ticking of a great clock, and it was all but drowned out by the thunder of battering rams at the far gates above.

"It continues," Max said softly.

Turning aside, Relna waved her hand, and a portion of the wall shifted aside. A pack of large red wolves raised their heads in an inside chamber.

"Come," said Relna, and the wolves padded toward her.

The queen faced her daughter. "The bonds of family cannot be forgotten, even in war," she said, wiping her daughter's cheek. "Dear, I love you."

Keeah, her eyes wet, held her mother the way Eric's mother had held him.

The largest of the red wolves murmured, and the queen nodded. "It is time. Good luck. Keep hope. Be safe."

With a rustle of her cloak, she was gone.

The wolves wasted no time, trotting quickly from passage to passage, slowing at each corner to listen before continuing.

Finally, the lead wolf stopped, tilted its head, pricked up its ears, and growled softly.

Keeah nodded. "I understand. Thank you."

She took two steps to the right and opened a small wooden door. Inside were carpets, some stacked, others rolled and standing up, still others spread out and hovering several inches above the floor.

"Pasha's workroom!" exclaimed Max. "His hidden workshop! Who knew it was here?"

The little inventor jumped up from behind a tall stack of carpets and embraced the children. "Oh, it's been so long since our last meeting. I hear you must flee."

"Not by choice," said Keeah. "The skies are filled with wingwolves, so unfortunately carpets are out of the question. We need to travel swiftly by land to Bangledorn."

Pasha stroked the long ends of his mustache. "Hmm . . . mm . . . wait, I have just the thing!" He opened a closet door and wheeled out a vehicle that was as outlandish as it was familiar.

"Your sand cycle!" said Neal. "I've always loved that thing!"

"It hasn't been raced since we were in Doobesh together," said Pasha. "Or washed, I might add."

"Washed or not, I claim shotgun!" said Julie, nudging Neal aside and hopping into the front seat of the sidecar.

Everyone piled onto the creation's various seats and platforms. With a chuckle, Pasha revved up the motor, steered it out the door, and in a flash, the entire band of friends was roaring through the tunnels. A few minutes later, they popped up outside the walls, behind enemy lines.

"It's Sparr," said Keeah, pointing up. "He's got a good lead, but wingwolves are not far."

When Eric saw the swarm growing behind Sparr, he knew Gethwing would soon suspect the worst — that Eric had betrayed him, that he was no longer Prince Ungast. Then the real battle between them would begin.

And the prophecy — the strange, incomplete, and long-hidden prophecy, whatever it meant — would come true.

What about the one?

"The moon is dropping quickly," said Max, crowding next to Neal. "The dawn of the last day approaches soon. Too soon."

The first hour passed quickly, then a second. Pasha's vehicle raced at top speed, but the distance was great. Finally, they arrived at the edge of the great and mysterious darkness of tall trunks and tangled branches.

"The Bangledorn Forest," whispered Julie. "It was here that I was scratched by the wing-wolf and first gained powers."

Eric dismounted and stepped slowly toward the black trees. In shadow now, the forest was a great living city where no magic was permitted.

"We're not alone here," whispered Keeah. "I sense something moving inside, and I don't mean the monkey folk. There are other forces at work here. Dark forces."

"You're beginning to scare me," said Julie.

Neal burst out laughing. *"Beginning* to scare you? I've been terrified since I woke up this morning!"

"I shall hide the sand cycle nearby and guard it with my life," Pasha said.

"Thank you," said Keeah.

Max took a step gingerly into the woody darkness. "Slow and steady, friends. Let us delay no more. Let us rather take heart, keep hope, remain calm, and — oh!"

Branches snapped, leaves crashed, there was a streak of orange hair flying upward, and Max was nowhere in sight!

"What —" cried Julie.

More tree limbs crackled, and *she* was gone!

Neal was nothing but a blur of blue turban when he vanished.

Keeah spun around, then flew up and away into the branches. "Eric, help!"

"Oh, you'll get help!" whispered a voice.

"But not from Eric!" whispered a second.

Before he could move, Eric's feet were yanked out from under him with a harsh tug, and he was pulled straight up into the darkness of the trees.

"Whoa! WHOA! HEY —"

Seven

In the Green Paradise

The children were yanked high up into the branches. They thrashed, flailed, and struggled to escape, when they heard the voices again.

"Hush, friends. The woods have ears!"

"And eyes!" said the second.

"And claws!" said the first.

Eric craned his neck and managed to look directly overhead. Peeking slyly out from the leafy branches above him were two small faces edged in green fur. Their eyes were large and brown, their noses like round brown buttons, their ears enormous, and their smiles broad and friendly.

"Twee?" said Neal. "Is that you?"

"And Woot?" said Julie.

"Present and accounted for!" chirped the green-furred monkeys the children had met twice before.

"Our dear forest friends," said Keeah. "Are we glad to see you!"

"Alas, our forest is full of *unfriendly* creatures, too," said Twee.

"Full of strangers and dangers," Woot added. "But we'll be your guides. Follow us to Queen Ortha's watchtower. Hurry."

"And be silent as monkeys!" said Twee.

The children were unbound in an instant, and together the friends flitted through the trees, leaping from one vine to another to another, hundreds of feet above the forest floor.

It was clear that things had changed greatly since their last time in the Bangledorn empire. Some trees were burned, others broken, still others blasted as if by explosions. Here and there towers of smoke rose through the leaves from the narrow pathways below.

"This is Ortha's secret lookout," said Twee.

They came to rest on a high, roofed platform wedged into the fork of a tall flowering tree. A bamboo curtain clattered, and then the tall, majestic ruler of Bangledorn entered.

"Welcome, guests," Queen Ortha said. Her voice was low yet strong. "Enemies have forced us into the uppermost branches."

Ortha was strong and noble of character, a mighty leader to her people, but her regal face was lined with worry and fear. The children had never seen her with armor on. It was made of sticks entwined to form an impenetrable mesh, overlaid with a weave of thick, dry leaves that shone like coins.

"That's why we're here," said Eric. "We're on a quest." *The final quest*, he said to himself.

"The Hakoth-Mal — those terrible and strong-winged wolves — have set up camps everywhere among the trees," Woot said, fear welling in his large eyes. "Each day they are making inroads into our homeland."

"And scaring the little folk," Twee added. "Much littler than us even!"

Keeah breathed deeply. "We're on a quest to stop the conquest of Droon. To do that, we must find the Temple of Zara."

Max nodded. "Lord Sparr may already have found the temple. He has his brother Urik's magic wand."

Twee gulped nervously. "But her temple lies in the eastern sector."

"Where the enemy presence is thickest and night is deepest," said Woot. "Our poor eastern cousins are afraid and in hiding."

Ortha motioned to the darkest part of the forest. "Magic is forbidden here. Be careful what you do. Your journey will not be an easy one. You must travel through the canopy of treetops, then down among the largest of the wingwolf camps. The Temple of Zara has been abandoned for weeks. Even the *droomar*, those ghostly elfin helpers of old, could not stay in their posts. Our forest is becoming one of the Dark Lands."

The children looked at one another.

"And yet . . . ," said Keeah. She drifted off. "Wait. Eric, what are you looking at?"

He stood at the edge of the platform, gazing down into the moving darkness. It was lit here and there by the green torchlight of the beasts. He recalled what he'd seen from Gethwing's back hours before. His spirits sank ever lower. "Even if we continue, time is running away from us. I can't believe —"

"You must believe," Ortha interrupted. "And you must go now. Eric, where there are friends, there is hope. I myself await reinforcements from Jaffa City. Perhaps you know them. The purple Lumpies?"

"Of course, we know them!" said Neal. "Khan is one of our best friends."

"Without his help, we shall lose our forest altogether," said Woot. "And when our forest goes, then goes . . . everything."

Eric breathed out. *The end of days . . .*

"That won't happen," said Keeah.

"Absolutely not," said Julie.

"No way," said Neal. "We still have . . . twelve hours."

"And that, too, is hope," the forest queen said. She stooped to embrace them all, ending in a long and wordless hug with Keeah.

With the duo of normally playful monkeys leading them, the five friends trekked from tree to tree, sometimes swinging down to the ground and racing as quickly and quietly as possible to the next tangle of vines.

Soaring up to a broad tree limb, the friends paused to catch their breath.

"They say monsters already dwell among the next trees," Woot whispered. "I fear we will not get close —"

Leaves whooshed suddenly, and a small face appeared in the branches.

"Cousin!" said Twee and Woot together.

With a swift loop of its tail around a vine, a third little monkey swung over to them.

"My name is Weaf!" she said, extending a slender paw to Keeah. "Pleased to meet you. I live in the eastern woods. Well, I *used* to live in the eastern woods — before those terrifying wolves took over. But there is still a way in."

Scanning the branches this way and that, Weaf pressed a finger to her lips and motioned for them to follow.

As quietly as they could, they climbed from branch to branch, and then slid down vine after vine until they reached the forest floor.

"A zig, a zag, and here we are!" said Weaf.

And there they were, in view of a tree stouter and taller than any other in the forest.

"The Dream Tree," Keeah whispered.

Though they could not see it yet, they knew that beneath the Dream Tree stood the Temple of Queen Zara, mother of the wizard dynasty.

"I smell wingwolves," said Julie. "Everyone be on guard."

"The wolves are not our only worry!" said Woot. "Look what Twee just found!"

The children crowded around the little monkey. In his palm he held a shiny object the size of a quarter.

"A dragon scale?" said Neal.

"Is Gethwing here?" asked Keeah.

Eric shuddered at the mention of the dragon's name. He didn't want to be found yet, especially not in the company of his friends.

"And this," said Weaf. "A scorched branch. It is a fire-breathing dragon. The worst kind!"

There was a sudden explosion of flames just beyond the clearing. A pilka whinnied.

"Back, you fiend!" cried a voice.

"It's Sparr!" yelled Neal. "That fire-breathing dragon is after him —"

The children tore quickly through the trees, where Sparr, managing to free himself from the dragon, joined them.

"I neared the temple of my mother," he said breathlessly. "But I could not get in. It is wound in ancient spells I cannot pierce. Besides that, it appears to be guarded by a dragon! Poor Kem ran off —"

"I smell something," said Neal.

"Neal," Julie said. "Are you seriously thinking of food at a time like this?"

"Naturally," said Neal. "But it's not what you think. I smell someone . . . baking something."

"Not the monkeys," said Woot. "We have strict orders to stay hidden, and that means no cooking or baking or fires of any kind."

Leaves thrashed among the trees behind them. Sparr wheeled around. "The dragon comes again. Prepare to defend ourselves —"

All at once, a great green dragon stomped out of the dense woods and roared, snorting a huge cloud of fire at the children.

"On him!" cried Sparr.

The moment the dragon appeared, lashing out with claws as long as sword blades, Kem galloped into the clearing. "Roo-oooo —"

The dragon turned suddenly at the sound. It lost its footing, stumbled backward, and fell to the ground with a thud. "Ohhhh!"

The instant it did, its mighty horned head shrank to the size of a melon. Its massive claws dwindled to a set of paws with close-cropped nails.

"Do not hurt him!" the dragon cried. "Little king! Poor little king! Poor him . . ."

"Jabbo?" the children shouted together.

The plump dragon blinked, and then pulled itself up from the ground. "Friends? You recognize poor Jabbo from days gone by?"

It *was* Jabbo, king of the city of Doobesh and former pie maker to Salamandra, queen of thorns.

"No wonder I smelled food," said Neal. "Jabbo, you were baking!"

"He was," said Jabbo, who always spoke about himself in the third person. "Jabbo is a pie maker, once again. He and his fog pirates were forced from Doobesh when that evil

Princess Neffu attacked. Then he had a dream that told him to guard the Temple of Zara. It's where he learned a special recipe to turn him into a vicious creature. It was a dream he simply had to obey!"

"That's why you were scary and green," said Julie. "You transformed yourself with your pies!"

Sparr stroked his beard. "A dream, you say? And it told you to come here? To the Dream Tree?"

"It did," said the dragon, pulling his chef's hat over his crown. "And the voice in Jabbo's dream was a lady's voice."

"My mother's voice," Sparr said softly, gazing at his brother's wand, then at Eric. "She has brought us all here with magic in hand . . ."

"Roo-roo?" said Kem.

"Yes, Kem," said Sparr. "But speak so that others may understand."

"Our pleasure," said the dog. "We have

determined that the wingwolves have wound a nearly unbroken sequence of spells around the temple so that no one may find it."

"*Nearly* unbroken?" said Julie.

Both of Kem's sets of jaws smiled. "Just so. We have discovered a gap in their charms just big enough for a dog. Even a dog with two heads. And his friends! This way."

Kem stalked slowly among the thick growth toward the base of the great tree, then partway out again, then partway back, threading the band of friends silently through the wingwolves' twisted maze of spells. At last they parted a final wall of ragged vegetation and beheld the remains of the temple.

Keeah gasped. Sparr froze where he stood. Eric couldn't breathe.

The Dream Tree was enormous, far larger than any tree they had seen before. It towered above the friends, above the forest, even above Droon.

At its roots stood the ancient temple. One of its most arresting features was the great stone face of the queen who lay entombed inside and whose image Eric had last glimpsed on the figurehead of the stone ship.

Perhaps most astonishing, however, was the building itself.

The wood of the tree and the stone of the temple blended in such a way as to become one, and whether roots grew from the temple or the temple had set out roots was unclear. The two things — tree and stone — were so twined into each other as to become a single living thing.

"The Dream Tree and the Temple of Zara," said Max softly.

Sparr sank to his knees at the sight of his mother's burial place. "I must enter the deepest chamber of her temple," he said. "I must see her."

In the silence that followed, and slowly, as slowly as the moon moves across the open sky, Sparr rose to his feet.

Raising his head, he stepped toward the crumbling temple stairs.

Silently calling the others to him and raising the glowing Wand of Urik, Lord Sparr ascended the ruined steps.

Eight

In the Temple Precincts

Drawn by the almost hypnotic way Sparr moved, the children slowly mounted the temple steps and passed behind the great, carved face of her to whom it was dedicated.

At first, all was dark.

Then, as if the old stones gave off their own dim light, the children began to see.

What they saw were walls broken by roots, smudged black with mold, and stained by five centuries of rain. Here and there a column that should have supported the high ceiling was cracked. In many places, the ceiling itself had fallen in, and debris was piled beneath its openings like so many altars of rubble.

Yet they, too, were beautiful. For the moonlight that penetrated the tangled tree branches overhead fell onto the crumbled stones with a silvery sheen.

"It's like entering a house of prayer," Julie whispered.

"I feel we are going back in time," said Keeah, "stepping hundreds of years into the mysterious past."

Hearing Sparr's unseen footsteps in the darkness before them, the children continued toward the inner court of the temple.

The past? thought Eric.

Of course.

Queen Zara was at the heart of the Droon adventure, just as her temple was at the heart of the Dream Tree and her Dream Tree at the heart of the forest.

It's right that we should be here, Eric reflected. *One last time.*

Ahead of them, they spied torches of silver flame, which must have been burning for years and years.

"The crypt," said Keeah, her voice hushed.

While they stood on the top step of a narrow staircase leading down, the children heard a terrible thrashing in the high trees above the temple.

"The wingwolves are outside," said Julie. "It sounds like a lot of them."

Hearing the slow progress of Sparr's footsteps below, the children hurried down the stone stairs. They crouched through a low tunnel and out into a room with a high, vaulted ceiling.

In the center, on a raised platform, stood a crystal coffin. Inside, like a fallen statue — silent, lifeless, unmoving — rested the body of Queen Zara.

As if made of stone himself, the gaunt sorcerer stood motionless over her.

"Sparr . . . ," Keeah whispered.

He did not stir.

"Look around," murmured Max, waving at what appeared to be curtains hanging down from the broken ceiling. They were not curtains but living things!

Spiders had woven webs all over the crypt. But each web was intricate and beautiful, undulled by the dust of ages, but quavering in the moonlight from above.

"Like jeweled necklaces," whispered Keeah.

"They are!" said Jabbo.

The webs *were* like jeweled necklaces, constructions of impossible complexity and strung from wall to wall to wall around the glass coffin like garlands of honor, casting a silvery glow upon her face.

Her face.

In the silence, Eric moved close enough to see the queen clearly. His heart fluttered and skipped. Under a length of sheerest fabric, a shroud no thicker than a glaze of frost, her features were pale, young, beautiful, and unmoving.

Eric drew in a long, silent breath.

The long-ago day when Julie was scratched by the wingwolf in the upper limbs of the Dream Tree was the same day he had descended to this very crypt.

The sender of dreams to all of them over the whole of their time in Droon, Zara — or her spirit — had spoken to him then, one-to-one, and given him the clearest vision of the future he had ever had.

It was a vision that overwhelmed all others.

In it, he saw a vast desert at dawn.

And they were there, all four of them, Julie, Neal, Keeah, and him. They rode four pilkas side by side at the head of a long, twisting caravan of hundreds.

Glistening on the horizon far, far in the distance stood a fabulous city bathed in golden light.

"It looks like a long journey," he had said to Zara then. She had not responded to that, and now, perhaps, he knew why.

The vision wasn't real. The journey would not happen, the quest was ending.

The final days had become the final day.

In a few short hours, it would all be over.

The golden light of his vision faded in the cold air, and everything was as before.

"Eric, hold out the Medallion," Sparr said. "It is time."

Eric did as he was asked, and the Medallion's light fell on the crystal coffin.

Raising the wand of his brother high overhead, Sparr spoke. "O, thou, youthful in age, unchanged since the instant of your passing, breathe . . . breathe . . ."

Softly at first, then more loudly, he spoke the words. He spoke them again and again until his voice rose to a crescendo, ending with the command, "Breathe, Mother! Breathe!"

Silence followed.

His vigor spent, Sparr collapsed. His hand fell to his side, and the wand slipped from its holder's fingers for a second time that day.

Also for the second time, Eric saved it at the last instant from striking the wet stone.

A single petal, loosed from the blossom at its tip, floated as though in an updraft of wind and settled ever so lightly on the queen's pale forehead.

Sparr drew in a quick breath and went still.

All went still in the cold stone room.

No one breathed.

Moments passed that seemed like hours.

All was silent.

Then . . . the fabric stirred.

The fabric stirred, and Eric felt ice run through his veins. The spiderwebs radiating from the coffin trembled like so much lace, and in that trembling made a sound like the chiming of tiny bells.

This music echoed in the stony room, and the fabric drew close over Zara's face.

Then it billowed out. In. Out.

"She's . . . breathing!" cried Keeah.

Zara stirred and rose at the same moment that Sparr raised his head. Their eyes met for the first time since her death five centuries before.

Eric and his friends were frozen where they stood. They watched Zara step from her crystal case and raise her arm to her son.

Without a pause, Sparr drew his mother close, and they embraced as they had not for centuries. Sparr fell to his knees a second time. "Mother — I —"

"Rise, son," she said, her voice as strong as it was tender, as full of power as it was gentle. "The hour has come for us to fulfill our ancient destiny — all of us. All of my sons."

Collect the magics . . .

Zara turned to the children, who one by one bowed to her. It was only then that Eric realized he was still holding Urik's wand. Hastily, he offered it to Sparr.

The sorcerer could not take his eyes from his mother. He did not seem to notice the wand.

"Queen Zara," said Eric, his heart stinging once more. "The wand of your son . . ."

She seemed about to say something, then simply smiled. "Eric, take it. For now."

"You sent us dreams," Keeah said. "Every single one of us had your dreams. Those dreams took us on a quest."

Zara nodded. "All of you — and others, too. Galen, for one. But that quest is not finished. We must find Galen now. Eric, you came here once. I spoke to you."

"I remember every word."

"Your stone in the great mosaic of wizards," she said.

"I remember that, too," he said, seeing a stone on the wall bearing his name in the old Droon language.

He touched the stone. Electricity coursed through his cold veins, warming him.

"And Urik's stone?" she said.

He touched it, too. It had the same effect.

"And mine," said Sparr, his eyes fixed on the stone with his symbol engraved upon it.

Zara moved her finger to another position on the wall. "And Galen's. Eric, touch it."

When he placed his finger on Galen's stone, it loosened and fell into his hand. A small rolled sheet of parchment was hidden in the space behind it. He took it out.

"Behold the first map Galen ever made in Droon," the queen said.

Scratched on the parchment was a drawing that again bore the unmistakable handiwork of Quill, Galen's magical feather pen. Several Droon landmarks were clearly marked. The icy range of the Tarabat hills, the mountain of Silversnow, the deserts of Lumpland — all were there.

At the far left edge of the parchment the western coast of Droon was sketched in, though sections of what would become the great royal capital of Jaffa City appeared as no more than meager settlements.

"The Dark Lands were so much smaller than they are now," said Keeah. "We've been losing the fight for Droon for a long time."

"As Galen searched for me," Zara said, "he and Quill drew in the places of this beautiful world. This world, that is now overcome with darkness. The time has come to turn back the Dark Lands."

"But how?" asked Julie. "The royal armies are in disarray. The beasts number in the millions. Galen is lost. Urik is lost. Gethwing is immortal. We are only this many."

"Then we need more. We need everyone. We need to collect the magics," Zara said.

The very words Eric had had in his mind since riding on Gethwing's back. "But how do we do this?"

"Hold the map to the light," said Zara. "Hold it up, and see a second map!"

As Eric held one side and Keeah took

the other, they held up the old map to the moonlight. Only when light shone through it did crisscrossing marks connecting distant places become visible. For an instant, Eric was reminded of the blank map at Zorfendorf.

But here, hundreds of such lines were drawn all across the world of Droon, from desert to city, from mountain to valley, from the darkest lands all the way to Jaffa City. Under Jaffa City, barely legible, was a nearly perfect circle with vague lines running from the outside in.

"What are all these lines?" said Julie. "What do they mean?"

"They are the threads that connect all things," said Zara, "no matter how distant in time or place they are."

"The Passages!" said Jabbo. "Of course!"

The Passages were tunnels under Droon's surface, connecting every part with every other part. They were magical, for one could enter a passage in one place and go almost instantly to a far distant part of the world.

"But why do we need the map?" asked Neal.

"Because deep in the Passages is where my lost son is," said the queen.

"Urik?" Eric said suddenly.

Zara turned to him, a mysterious look in her eyes. "Urik is lost where I, for one, cannot find him. Perhaps he is lost beyond all hope of finding. No, long ago Galen used the Passages to search for me. We will find him there —"

The howling of wingwolves came from nearby. It was answered with the clatter of sticks and the alarms of the tree monkeys.

"To the surface, quickly!" said Sparr.

As they hurriedly climbed the steps, Zara explained. "From my tomb, I sent Galen a dream. A thousand things must join to save Droon. In the Passages his quest takes place."

"So many quests," said Neal. "I've counted about a dozen so far. And they all have to be finished by dawn."

"Are you saying that Galen *wasn't* kidnapped?" said Julie. "That he vanished because of a dream you sent him?"

The queen nodded. "Not long ago, I saw an image of horns aflame, an image that pains me beyond belief. I sent Galen to find Ko."

"Emperor Ko?" said Keeah. "But he's . . . well, he's . . . dead."

"Ko died when Galen pushed him from the precipice near Silversnow," said Max.

"Ko may have died," said Zara, "but he is part of the battle for Droon, too. Ko has a vital piece of information we must know if we are to win back this world. Hurry, into the Passages. Time is leaving us. Droon is leaving us!"

Nine

Raising the Unwanted Dead

The battle had moved on by the time they emerged from the temple into the forest. The moon was directly overhead, and still their quest was unfinished.

"Midnight," said Sparr, looking at Eric. "Gethwing will surely return before dawn."

"And want me back," said Eric.

"Well, he can't have you," said Julie.

"I have to go back to him," Eric said. "Neal knows I do. He saw it in his vision. I'm with Gethwing at the very end."

"Fiddlesticks!" said Max. "In the next few hours the final assault on our beloved capital will take place. Our quest is far from over. As you say, we *must* collect the magics, and you are needed for that."

"Do you have to return to him?" asked Keeah, laying her hand on his arm.

"Soon," said Eric. "But not yet. We have Sparr, the wand, Queen Zara, but our quest isn't done. Galen's not here."

He knew another was not with them, either.

A sharp pain not unlike the one he had for Zara struck his heart when he realized that Urik would not join them.

Lost beyond all hope of finding.

Clutching the wand tightly, Eric wondered, rejected the idea, then wondered again: *Will I be called upon to play the part Urik would have played?*

And more than that — do I have any chance of succeeding?

* 130 *

The deep forest was quiet, the air momentarily clear of smoke.

"Where is the nearest entrance to the Passages?" asked Neal. "We need to get a move on."

Zara traced her fingers across Galen's map. "A grove of ancient oaks northwest of here."

Threading the forest paths quietly and carefully, they soon found a tight clearing surrounded by immense oak trees. Set in the midst of them was a shadowed place that signaled an entrance into the earth.

"In we go!" Max said.

"Him, too!" said Jabbo.

"Roo!" Kem added.

Though at first it appeared no larger than a rabbit hole, the tunnel easily accommodated the entire group. Zara and Sparr quickly took the lead, Max, Kem, and Jabbo on their heels. Neal and Julie went next, followed at last by Keeah and Eric.

Down, down, down they went. Before they had traveled far, they were met by a pair of heavily whiskered, four-footed creatures with pug noses and tufted brows.

"Mooples!" said Keeah.

"Friends!" the creatures chimed.

"We're happy to see you," said Eric.

"And you, too," said one, looking Eric up and down. "Although your scary armor makes us fear."

"There is plenty to fear," said Max, peering into the twisting tunnels ahead. "But not from Eric or Lord Sparr."

"Roo!" said Kem. "I mean, that's right."

Sparr turned. "My mother and I shall search the area ahead. One moment."

"We hear the most terrible things about the world on the surface," whispered the first moople. "Icky things. War and such."

"But that's not all," said the second. "There have been noises down here as well. And messages!" He handed them a scrap of paper.

It read: *Join me now!*

"Quill again!" said Max. "Galen is near!"

"Have you seen him?" Jabbo asked.

The two creatures frowned, mumbled together, then one spoke. "Chubby fellow, red costume, white beard, sack of toys?"

"Man, that guy gets around!" said Neal.

"No," said Keeah. "Cloak of midnight blue, tall cone hat, beard to his waist —"

"We saw him, too!" said the other. "Come!"

Joining Sparr and his mother, the little band followed the pair of mooples into the twisting depths. Scraping and scrabbling their way through the earthy tunnels, they came finally to a crossroads where three paths met.

"Oh, dear," whispered the pie maker. "Jabbo's poor toes begin to tingle!"

"What does that mean?" asked Julie.

"That he forgot to powder his toes again," said Jabbo. "But also — look there!"

Eric raised Urik's glowing wand toward the shadows when all at once the left-hand passage whirled with a storm of flying thorns.

Sparr stood fast, his fingers spread wide, blue sparks sizzling on their tips.

"Enemy or friend?" he demanded.

"Is there a third choice?" came the reply, and out of the shadows stepped a young woman, her thorny hair in constant motion.

"Salamandra! Ruler of Pesh!" shrieked Jabbo, huddling behind Max and Kem.

"Queen of Shadowthorn, it is, my chubby pie maker!" she said with a deep bow as she clutched her thorn-tipped staff at her side. "Though after this, I'm thinking Empress!"

Zara raised her eyebrows. "After what?"

"After . . . this!" she said. "Oh, yoo-hoo!"

From the darkness behind her came a whisper. "Hello? Friends? Mother —"

"It's Galen!" Max shouted.

"Galen!" said Keeah.

"My son!" gasped Queen Zara.

They all rushed into the darkness and pulled Galen to them. His mother embraced her son as if she never wanted to be parted again. Neither had seen the other for centuries.

Finally, Zara pulled back, and Galen and his younger brother Sparr hugged as Eric had never seen them do. He, Julie, Keeah, and Neal joined them.

The homecoming could have lasted longer, but Zara spoke. "There is much to say, much to feel and remember," she said softly. "But not now. War does not cease above us. Time does not stop."

"Oh, time'll stop, all right," said Salamandra. "When the old guy does his little trick."

"Hush, thorn queen," said Galen, turning to the others. "Days and nights it took, and the thorn queen's special talents, but I have found what I needed to. Come, everyone. See." He plunged back into the darkness.

Salamandra smirked. "You all thought Galen was kidnapped, didn't you? Well, sorry to disappoint you. He simply chose an ally no one would ever suspect. To tell you the truth, it even surprised me! Come on. See what we found. This way."

"Here we take our leave," the mooples said. They bowed and retreated into the depths of the Passages.

"Little folk must stick together," said Jabbo, still clutching Max. "You and Jabbo. Yes?"

"Yes, indeed," said Max. "Come along."

"Us four!" said Kem, poking both heads between them and trotting along.

Zara, Sparr, Keeah, Eric, Neal, and Julie followed close behind and soon came to a place of hazy light.

Eric knew in an instant where they were. He looked up, but saw only a vague blue glow. Far above and out of sight of the passage below stood the great dome where he was wounded and cursed by Ko.

The mystery of what happened there had never left him, and his mind whirled with thoughts of Galen and Sparr and Urik, and of the blue serpent that he was sure had become an airplane just before it vanished.

A breath over his shoulder made him turn.

Zara's face had drained of color until she seemed no more than a ghost. The reason was clear. In the shadows just beyond the light lay an unmoving form.

It was the evil one.

Emperor Ko, the gargantuan bull-headed creature with three eyes and four arms and two coiled horns, lay sprawled at the bottom of a ravine in a heap of twisted limbs.

"Begging your pardon," said Max, "but it serves him right. Bad man . . . bull . . . thing!"

"Beast," Zara said. "The cause of so much pain. And death. The anguish of centuries —"

Ko's curse, based on its own prophecy, had nearly killed Eric. The sons of Zara were to be in one place, where one would fall. But hadn't the prophecy been wrong, after all? The sons of Zara were not together.

The third man had been the Prince of Stars, not Urik. And Eric had fallen instead.

Not Urik. Only the Prince of Stars, the man with no memory.

"And yet, sweet mother," said Galen, "we

must bring Ko back. For only he can tell us where Gethwing's wheel of life is."

"Listen to your long-bearded son," said Salamandra. "Let him bring the beast back. Let Ko's memory live once more."

Memory. No memory. Time. No time.

All things connect.

Eric's mind reeled with confusion.

With a swirl of her staff, Salamandra scattered a handful of thorns in a circle around the lifeless form. "Time, turn 'round."

Without warning, Ko's body rose slowly from its heap. The crushing impact of its striking the earth reversed itself, and Ko seemed to struggle back to life.

His great mouth opened in a silent scream, and his arms flew upward.

"I don't believe this!" said Max.

"Believe it!" said Jabbo. "He has seen mighty magic from the queen of thorns."

Ko moved slowly up through the air and back toward the surface from which he'd fallen.

Galen's hands rose suddenly. "Cease!" he said, and Ko hung suspended in the air.

Eric, Keeah, Neal, Galen, and Sparr all worked together to erect a prison around Ko.

Iron bars of sizzling flame wound around the horned beast. Ko, as if awaking from his own death, growled and beat his chest with his four giant fists like a captive ape.

"I . . . AM . . . KO!"

Zara stared at him, saying nothing.

But other eyes caught Eric's attention. Salamandra was looking at him, and his last meeting with her rushed back into his mind. With her usual mischief, she had spoken a strange word to him as if it meant everything.

Reki-ur-set.

Was it nonsense, meant to drive him crazy? Or were all things truly connected and the strange word yet another clue, one among many pieces in the great puzzle of Droon?

He moved closer, her eyes still fixed on his. "What does it mean?" he asked. "The word."

A thin smile crossed her lips. "The word? It's a word, no more, no less."

"Words are magic," Eric said. "I know that."

"Well, yeah!" Salamandra said. "This one's even in your language. But I already told you that. It's just letters, letters written on water. Or air." She twirled her fingers in front of his face.

"On water or air!" he whispered, annoyed by Salamandra's riddles. "So what? What are you talking about?"

But Salamandra spun around to Galen. "Wizard, first foe of the beast emperor, first to vanquish him and make him sleep, work your magic now. Let us see what we need to see!"

Galen drew in a long slow breath. Pressing his hands together, he turned his palms upright. Out of them grew a light that enveloped first Ko, then the three wizards, then all of them, including Max, Jabbo, and Kem.

"We are in his memory now," said Galen. "Hush. Look. See."

Images formed in the air from the dim light. Rocky walls replaced the earthen passage. Green flame. The smell of dampness, then of cold, bitter cold.

A place far colder than this!

"I know this place," Neal whispered. "It's the Cave of Night. It's where Gethwing was born, but no one knows where it is!"

"Ko does," said Galen. "He shall show us."

In the image of the mysterious Cave of Night, Ko stood alone. Then in a flutter of wings, another entered.

It was Gethwing, no more than a fledgling.

"Weary miles brought me to this . . . place," said Ko, gazing around. "East beyond the light, west behind the shadow, north of the farthest valley, south of the tallest peak."

"This is where I was born," said Gethwing, his four young wings rustling nervously. "The mystery of my birth is here."

The dragon's suspicious eyes scanned the emperor, then the darkness behind him.

"We are well hidden, four wings," said Ko. "Never mind that. I am Ko, emperor of beasts. You are . . . a fledgling. Why have you asked me here, so far from my throne, and so cold?"

Gethwing bowed his head slightly, then raised it. His eyes flashed slightly. "There was a prophecy set in stone on the night of my birth. It concerns me and how I shall always be. Alive in the ashes. Alive at the end of days." He spoke in the age-old tongue. "*Muhtah-kef-thala-n'beth-kee . . . mor-pesla-nof-sullah-nem . . . ped-tronosh-kutcho-tha!*"

Understanding the ancient words, Eric heard the prophecy again.

Five shall pass away, four shall wear the crown, three shall fall, two shall rise together . . .

Gethwing stopped short of finishing.

Still no mention of the one!

Salamandra chuckled and leaned in to Eric. "You know, I've always had a problem with ancient prophecies. Traveling in time like I do, ancient is no big deal. Plus, different people read prophecies differently, you know?"

Eric turned to see her wink at him. "Huh? I'm trying to understand this —"

"Well, excuse me!" she said, and made a gesture of zipping her lips closed.

"Though it be centuries from this day," Gethwing told Ko, "and much must happen first, I am present at the end. The prophecy says so. I thought you would be interested. I thought you might be the other that *shall rise together* with me. That's all."

"The end of days?" said Ko, his three eyes glowing bloodred. "It's always been my dream to be there." And the frightening face contorted into a smile. "Together, then."

With that, the emperor held out a claw. The dragon raised his own. They touched, and a tongue of green fire erupted from them.

Eric knew what happened next.

The rise of Ko and Gethwing. Centuries of war. The great battle when Ko was wounded.

The charm that put Ko to sleep. How Gethwing was defeated, but could not die.

How Gethwing proved immortal.

Then, as the two beasts left the Cave of Night, claw in claw, the children saw it.

"Holy cow!" said Keeah.

"No kidding!" said Eric. "A place far colder . . . of course!"

Still within Galen's spell, inside Ko's memory, they saw the land outside Gethwing's cave. And just above the horizon was a lighted orb. A planet. It had rivers and valleys and ice mountains and sandy deserts.

"It's . . . Droon," said Keeah.

"Which means . . ."

"The Cave of Night is on Droon's moon!" said Neal. "I so knew that!"

"You *knew* that?" asked Julie.

"No," said Neal. "Didn't have a clue."

The friends gathered in the glow of the orb, even as it faded, and they were in the Passages once more, with Ko in his fiery prison.

"There is only one sure way I know to get to the moon," Sparr said to his mother.

"My flying chariot," said Zara.

"Our quest moves to the Forbidden City of Plud," said Galen. "Though it is a stronghold of the wicked wraiths now, we go into the Dark Lands. In stealth, in power, in haste!"

There was a sudden clattering behind them, and Jabbo shouted.

"No, no! Halt! Stop! Do not take him!"

With a sharp laugh, Salamandra twirled her staff, and thorns flew up around her.

"A Portal of Ages!" Keeah cried. "Salamandra, what are you doing?"

"You heard the prophecy, dearies," the thorn queen said. "Ko is around at the end."

"You can't!" shouted Eric, rushing at Salamandra. "Traitor!"

She stuck her tongue out at Eric, laughing. "And the chubby little pie maker, too. Buh-bye!" With that, she, Ko, and Jabbo vanished together in a storm of spinning thorns.

"Traitor, indeed!" said Galen, whipping his

cloak around angrily. "She used my magic to bring the evil one back to life! Now we must battle him as well! Our quest lengthens as our enemies increase and our time dwindles!"

"Poor Jabbo," said Max.

Kem rooed softly to himself.

"No one said it would be easy," said Neal. "But does it have to be this hard?"

There was no answer for his question.

Yet as the moon began to drop toward the horizon and the sky opposite to lighten from black to the deep blue of coming dawn, everyone thought the same thing.

No time!

No time!

Ten

Mysteries and Secrets

The Dark Lands were clearly visible when the little group reached the eastern edge of the forest. Massive clouds blacker than the night sky hung low over the land.

In the far distance stood the crooked shape of a tower, a symbol of evil, a place of terror.

"The Forbidden City of Plud is where Gethwing plans to set up shop," said Eric.

"He will never," said Sparr. "My home will not be defiled by that dark dragon —"

As if he'd heard his name uttered, Gethwing swept slowly across the distant sky, silhouetted against the approaching dawn.

Ice seeped into Eric's veins. "He's looking for me, wondering where I am."

"Then we must hurry," said Sparr. "Or all will be lost."

The soft *putt-putt* of Pasha's sand cycle neared, and the vehicle slid to a stop at the edge of the woods.

"Armies stain the southern valleys," said the little man. "I had to do some quick driving to escape them, which, of course, I love to do!"

"Thank you, clever friend," said Galen. "We are leaving here as soon as we can. Our quest leads us through the hard country of the Dark Lands and straight to Plud."

Pasha's face went pale. "But that . . . that . . . oh, dear me . . ."

Inside Eric a fire began to burn. He slid his fingers into the pocket of his cloak, grasped the photo he carried there, and drew it out.

He studied the blue, scallop-winged airplane, the curved roof of an airport hangar behind it, the man in a white flying suit holding a white hat at his side.

Memory. No memory.

Time. No time.

The man was his great-great-great grandfather, one of the earliest aviators, a friend of the Wright brothers and a builder of planes.

And yet . . .

His heart skipped a beat.

On the roof of the hangar sat three birds.

The photo was black and white, but he could tell that one of the birds was neither black nor white, but another color.

A voice in his heart reminded him of the birds that delivered Galen's note. And the birds in the chamber at Zorfendorf. And the birds that he had seen long before in the ice caves of Krog.

He knew those birds.

And he knew what he had to do.

Slipping the photograph back into his cloak next to the Moon Medallion, he turned to Galen. "Collect the magics. You told me this. Queen Zara, all your sons must be together in this quest. They all have to be here."

The queen lowered her head. "Urik is lost. Lost from us, lost in time —"

"Maybe," Eric said. "But the wand was lost. And so were you. We found you. Besides, when someone is lost, you find him."

"Alas, my boy, not even I know when or where he is," said Sparr, "though we traveled the same paths of time for centuries."

Eric looked at his friends, at Sparr, Galen, and Zara. "Our band is incomplete. I have to find him. I have to go."

"But where?" asked Keeah.

"Home," Eric answered. "A secret lies there. I've pushed it away for too long."

"The stairs cannot help us this time," said Galen. "It would be too dangerous to reveal them now, with spies all around us."

"And the ship is in Jaffa City," said Julie.

Suddenly, the pair of friendly mooples popped their heads from the shadows.

"Excuse us!" said one. "But we'd like to remind you that our Passages can help!"

"We're actually due to visit our cousins very near the capital," added the other.

"Use the wand if you must," said Zara, clasping her hands over Eric's. "You may need it. Urik's magic was — is — powerful, deep, and mysterious." She stopped. "Find him?"

"I'll try," said Eric.

Keeah wrapped her arms around him. "You know."

Pulling away, Eric smiled. "I know."

"Plus, good luck," said Neal, giving him a nudge on the shoulder.

"I don't know if luck has much to do with it," Eric said. "But thanks. I'll take it."

They stood for a moment longer, then Zara took a breath. "To Plud and my chariot!"

"And the wraiths!" added Max.

A minute later — *whoosh!* — Eric was hurtling through the Passages with the mooples.

Coiling tunnels stretched out and collapsed on him, but he kept moving until he shot out into the main plaza at Jaffa City.

"A spy!" screeched a voice. "Stop him!"

At once, arrows grazed the stones at his feet and whizzed past his ears.

"Keep your head down, and follow my light!" shouted King Zello, waving a lantern from behind a barrier of loose stones.

His mind a blur of fear and determination, Eric ran straight to the fountain. He leaped onto the deck of the stone ship, grasped the Medallion, and spun the wheel sharply. In a flash, the ship plummeted away from the city and into the earth below, its hull twisting and falling heavily into a river of silver water.

Wave after wave drove the ship on, faster and faster, until the water suddenly dropped away. The ship hung for a moment, and then plunged into a black underground sea. It rose up instantly, becalmed in the dark water.

The only sound was Eric's labored breathing

as he stood fast at his position at the wheel. His mind was filled with words.

Three shall fall. Gethwing said Ko and Zara were two of them. But they were both alive now. So who? Galen, Urik, and Sparr?

And if that part of the prophecy wasn't clear, what about the *two*? Two shall rise together? *Maybe it's not Gethwing and me. Maybe it's Gethwing and Ko.*

And *one.* What about the *one*?

I still don't know the one!

Wind howled suddenly through the cavern behind him, darkness fell, and the ship was propelled sharply forward.

Into a wall of rushing water. Going up!

"A waterfall!" he gasped. "Except it's not falling!"

Powerless to prevent the forward motion of the ship, Eric threw chains about the main mast and linked his arms through them.

The stone ship crashed into the watery wall, then flew straight up until there came an earth-shattering explosion of stone and water and he was hurtled out of the boat, through the air, and into silence.

For a moment.

Then there was nothing but noise.

When he opened his eyes, he was in a cloud of gauzy light.

The sharp, scorched scent of fresh-sawn wood filled his nose, and he heard a sudden hammering of nails, a motor's rough sputtering, and the calls of men, one to another, somewhere beyond him.

"What is going on?" he said. "Where am I?"

When the haze began to clear in a slant of early morning sun, he made out the large silhouette of a building.

"My house!" he gasped.

It *was* his house, though it was different than he knew it to be. "The upstairs dormer isn't there. And that noise across the street. That's Julie's house . . . just being built!"

Stepping carefully across his backyard, he saw the apple trees — three of them — that grew outside his room. They were shorter, too. The tallest branch of the tallest tree was still several feet below his bedroom window.

"I've gone back in time," he whispered. "But to when? How long ago is this?"

He stopped moving.

There was a child sitting on a low branch in the tallest of the three trees. It was a little boy with golden curls. He wore blue pants and a blue jacket. As morning light glinted off the damp bark, the tree had a silver cast.

Eric knew that his own hair turned from blond to brown before he entered school.

"It's me. I must be . . . three years old."

Words came back to him that he had heard so long ago.

"A child with golden curls, sitting alone in a silver tree."

Who had said those words?

His heart nearly stopped when he remembered.

There was movement in the house, and he crouched quickly behind a bush. Peeking up, he saw a young woman's face peer out of a nearby window.

"Mom!" he gasped softly. His mother smiled at his younger self and then turned away, but only for moments before looking out and smiling again.

Eric knew what she knew. The tree's lower branches twisted together to make a clever little seat and a safe spot to sit, even for a boy so young.

With a fluttering of wings, a plain white bird settled in the top branch of the tree. Young Eric looked up and smiled. A second bird came, this one black. Then a third. Its feathers were red.

Eric trembled. Three small crows, one red, one white, one black. He knew them, and breath left his lungs. His head felt light. He felt like he was falling a great distance.

"Can it really be true?"

A brittle leaf crackled behind him.

Eric turned in his hiding place.

An old man — older than old and dressed in white — took a step and paused. The boy sitting in the silver tree saw him. "Hello there," he said.

"Hello," said the old man.

"Who are you?" asked the boy.

"Your great, great . . . great grandfather," said the man. "People call me . . . Eric."

"That's my name!" said the boy.

"I know," said the man. "I'm pretty sure your mother named you after me."

"You're old," said the boy.

"You have no idea," said the old man, with a soft chuckle. "I was born about . . . six hundred years ago. A long way from here."

The boy laughed. "Silly. You fly planes. Mommy said so."

"I do," said the man. He took a step toward the tree and put his hand on a silver branch.

Eric could not breathe when he saw the man's fingers on the tree. Like a lightning flash, the word returned to him.

Reki-ur-set.

And a kind of smoky ink magically seeped from the wand's blossom and spelled the word in the air before him.

"My favorite was a blue plane," the man said. "I built it myself and called it the *Blue Serpent*."

"Why did you call it that?"

"It had curved wings and flew fast," the man said. "Very fast. Until it crashed."

"Were you hurt?"

The man nodded. "I lost my memory. For a long while. But I always remembered you. And look. I brought you something. You might need it later." He placed an object in the boy's palm and closed his hand over it.

Little Eric peeked into his hand and squealed. "Oh, wow! Is this for me?"

"I've carried it around for a long time," said the man. "Now it's your turn. Keep it safe. You'll need it someday. We all will."

"You bet I'll keep it safe!" said the boy.

There was a noise from inside the house, and the sound of a door opening. The old man

shrank back behind a bush as Mrs. Hinkle appeared. "Eric. Time to come in now."

Little Eric leaped down from the tree. "Mommy, look what I have. There was a man!"

His mother looked across the yard but saw no one. She closed the door behind them.

Eric stood, looking from the man, who saw him now, to the tree, to the house, and back, and he was overwhelmed with the memory of what his little palm had closed over. "The Pearl Sea! You gave me the Pearl Sea!"

"And . . . ," said the man, wiping his cheek.

"And . . . you're . . . Urik," said Eric. "My great-great-great grandfather!"

The old man bowed his head for an instant. With a curious smile on his lips, he lifted a finger and drew it across the air. The letters that had lingered there since Eric first thought of them — *Reki-ur-set* — drifted like smoke, then rearranged themselves, vanishing here, reappearing there.

Reki-ur-set

became

Urik's tree

Like lightning shooting from place to place to place, Eric's mind connected all the thoughts he had carried with him since that day so many years before.

The old man, the precious gift in the tree, the moment Sparr said that Eric was "one of us," the pain in his chest whenever he spoke the name of Zara, the fragments of memory, the movie of the old pilot, the leather-bound book written by Urik that happened to be in his town's library, his powers, the names Urik and Eric, the silver tree itself . . .

"But how is this possible?" said Eric.

Urik bowed his head for a moment, wiped his eyes, and spoke. "I followed my brother Sparr from Pesh in Salamandra's Portal of Ages. From here to there, from then to then, I turned up in various centuries at various places, and always fought him for the Moon Medallion. Until once, catching me off guard, he got the better of me."

"Sparr took it," said Eric. "I remember that. At the airfield in the old movie. Later, he asked Demither about its power."

Urik nodded. "After Sparr stole the Medallion from me, I built an aircraft that could fly from the Upper World to Droon," he said. "As you can guess, it was a rocky ride. My plane, the *Blue Serpent*, crashed in the snows of northern Droon."

"I was there," said Eric. "It's where I was wounded."

"I was hurt, too," Urik said. "I lost my memory. I wandered Droon, kept to the shadows, took different guises, different names, some of them quite funny. Birds were my friends from ancient times. These three stayed with me the whole way."

The three birds in the tree nodded as if they understood, and Eric knew they did. In fact, the birds could talk. Their names were Otli, Motli, and Jotli.

"You were the Prince of Stars," said Eric.

"I was."

"You said you were searching for a child with golden curls sitting in a silver tree," Eric said. "It's the only thing you remembered."

Urik smiled. "You're a memorable kid."

Blushing, Eric smiled, too. "It makes sense now. Ko's curse on the sons of Zara would only happen when all three of you were there, and you *were* there: you, Galen, and Sparr were in the same place at the same time."

"You were there, too," said Urik. "You're also a son of Zara — hundreds of years later. That's why you were struck and cursed."

"And why I'm here now," said Eric. "But how are you related to my mom?"

Urik smiled. "I told you Sparr caught me off guard? Well, there was a reason. A sweetheart."

"Really?" Eric asked.

Urik nodded. "Unable at first to get to Droon,

I stayed here after my fight with Sparr and married her. We had a child who had a child and so on, until your mother. All the way from my mother to you."

Eric wondered what his mother would say when he told her. Then he realized that there was something he needed to say. "It always hurt when I spoke Zara's name, but maybe not so much now, because . . . your mother is alive again."

Urik went pale. "I hoped with all my heart that it might happen. So. I have to return. I know Droon is going dark. I am a son of the Queen of Light. I think I can help a little."

"You can help a lot!" said Eric. "Droon needs you more than anything!"

"You, too. So I guess we'd better get going. And I think I know a good way." Urik held up a small, curved brown object.

Eric blinked and took the object into his fingers. "Are you serious? Is this one of Salamandra's thorns?"

Urik grinned. "I snitched it from the last time portal I was in. Maybe we can make a little portal right now. One just big enough to get us to Droon in time to save it."

"A mini Portal of Ages?" said Eric. "I love it! Let's take it right to Plud. That's where everyone is."

"Reunion time," said the old wizard.

"Here," said Eric. "Your wand. It belongs with you."

"Thanks," Urik said. "It feels good to hold it again."

With his wand in one hand and Salamandra's magic thorn in the other, Urik drew a wide circle around them. Instantly, the air grew dark, wind began to blow, and they were lifted up from the ground.

"Droon — ho!" they cried together.

Eleven

The Wraiths of Wrath

No sooner had the thorny portal begun to spin than Eric's backyard, his house, and his town all vanished.

"Hold — tight!" shouted Urik.

With no warning, the pair spun around like figure skaters, then tumbled down in a frightening free fall until the thorns cleared and they saw the crooked black tower of Plud.

It was coming up fast.

"Uh-oh!" cried Eric. With both hands

extended, he blasted the air below them, slowing their fall.

At the same time Urik waved his wand. A sudden updraft of wind pushed them sideways onto the tower. They rolled to a stop inches from the edge.

Urik laughed. "Not bad."

"No, it's bad," said Eric. "We're not alone."

A band of enraged wraiths burst from their guard posts, and sizzling laser-sharp beams exploded at Eric and Urik. They ducked behind a battlement and answered with their own barrage of sparks. A swarm of sword-wielding wraiths roared up from below to aid their friends.

"Wraith sandwich," Urik said, firing a wide spray of blue sparks. "Sometimes escape is the boldest course of action! Shall we flee?"

"I wouldn't have it any other way," said Eric.

Linking arms, the two raced to the edge of the tower and jumped.

Wham! They landed on the roof of the tower just below them. It was steeply pitched, and they slid off and landed even harder on the balcony beneath.

Though Eric knew exactly how old Urik was, their travel in the Portal of Ages seemed to have made him younger. As soon as they had landed on the balcony, Urik leaped to his feet and scanned the jagged walls below.

"Roof by roof to the ground?" he said.

"Good plan," said Eric. Then he heard the clash of weapons far below and spied a handful of tiny shapes race down the black stones of a narrow alley.

"It's Galen," he said. "He and the others are making for the rear courtyard, and so should we. Strength in numbers, I always say."

"A good saying," said Urik. "And one our enemies seem to know, too. Another band of wraithy guys just appeared on the north wall. The next roof looks like our only hope."

"In my mind I'm already there," said Eric.

But their escape was suddenly blocked when a fourth squad of wraiths poured out from the tower and onto the roof below.

The two wizards spun on their heels. Across the balcony stood two doors leading inside. Pointing to one then the other, Urik mumbled something, then nodded.

"This one!" Urik lunged at the door, flung it open, and pulled Eric inside.

It was dark and quiet.

Until there was a sudden flash of steel.

"Please don't tell me we picked the wrong door," said Eric.

"Okay," said Urik. "But I really hate to lie." He yanked Eric back out the door, and they jumped again and landed hard again.

"Children, behind us to the chamber!" Sparr yelled below. He and Kem stood fast at a corner, facing a dozen charging wraiths.

"I guess it's too much to hope that we run out of tower soon," said Eric.

"They build them tall in the Dark Lands," said Urik. "Going down again!"

They clambered down the face of the tower until they saw a slender opening in the wall.

"Our escape route?" asked Eric.

Arrows flew at them from above and below, pinging the stones around them.

"I'm willing to think so," said Urik.

Together they squeezed through the opening and somersaulted into a dark room, tumbling over objects until they came to a complete stop.

"I think we did it," whispered Urik.

"You did it, all right," growled a low voice.

Eric groaned. "Can't we catch a break?"

Torches flared to reveal a roomful of vicious snakelings.

"Apparently not here," said Urik.

The two wizards backed up step by step, until they felt the wall behind them.

"We get you," said one snakeling.

"We get you good," said another.

"Droon will fall," said the first.

"Droon will fall good," said the other.

"You talk too much," Urik said, then he whispered out of the side of his mouth, "On the count of three, ready?"

"Three!" shouted Eric.

The two wizards plowed right through the crowd of snakelings and out the door into the inner castle. No sooner had they slid down a banister onto the floor than the surrounding walls started to move. Toward them.

"Are those walls trying to crush us?" asked Urik.

"I hate when that happens!" said Eric. "Sparr rigged Plud to trap his enemies. And in those days *everyone* was his enemy —"

All at once, the walls jerked to a noisy stop, one shifted aside, and there were Kem and Sparr, grinning at Eric and Urik.

"Come with me if you want to live!" Sparr said.

"That's *my* line!" said Urik. The two brothers slapped each other on the back and laughed until Eric pushed them both into the hallway. "Party later, guys. We gotta move."

"There," said Sparr. "To the secret chamber!" And he zigzagged through the castle's passages as if threading an incomprehensible maze only he knew the plan of.

Soon they were in a room with Galen, the children, Max, and Queen Zara. Urik's homecoming brought an explosion of cries and hugs.

"My son!" cried Zara.

"My brother!" said Galen.

They clutched one another, howling and weeping. When Urik broke away long enough to tell everyone who Eric really was, Eric felt his heart rise into his throat, and he began to cry himself.

His friends and family instantly wrapped around him, nearly knocking him to the floor with weeping and laughing.

The reunion didn't last long, however. It *couldn't* last long, for the room echoed with the sudden flutter of bird wings.

"Danger!" said Otli. "A fresh squad of wraiths is on its way."

"Hurry to the secret chamber!" said Jotli.

"We think now is a good time!" said Motli.

"Roooo!" said Kem.

With Sparr in the lead, the band of friends rushed through the passages from one level to the next and finally met a wall in which there was no door. It was not, however, a dead end.

Speaking soft words once, twice, three times, Sparr stood back. The wall slid aside soundlessly.

"Handy if you know the combination," said the sorcerer. "Step inside, if you please."

The children had seen the secret chamber once before. Like that first time, they stood before a magical horse-drawn chariot made entirely of hammered silver.

"I fashioned this long ago," said Zara, running her hands along its railing, "for you and me together, my youngest son. Little did I know that neither of us would ever ride in it."

"Until now," said Sparr. He helped his mother climb aboard her magical chariot, then slid a sword from a crest on its front. It made a clean whistling sound when he twirled it.

"Armed and ready," he said.

Galen and Urik took their places with their mother. The children, Max, and Kem leaped in last.

"And now to Parthnoop," said Neal. "I hear the bad guys coming —"

Wham! Stone blocks blew aside, and the room filled with wraiths and snakelings.

"No time to lose!" said Galen. "Eric, the Medallion!"

Eric drew the silver Medallion from his cloak and inserted it into the chariot's crest.

At once, the horse came alive. Its great wings swept wide. On Zara's command, the creature raised its front legs high and clawed the air with a flash of hooves. The wraiths fell back for only an instant, but it was long enough.

With a swift *shoosh!* the chamber walls separated, and the chariot shot out to the cobblestones of the courtyard. The horse leaped for the sky, and the chariot flew.

The friends zoomed up through the silver air, heading directly for the distant moon. But before they had flown far, the air shuddered with angry wings.

"The Hakoth-Mal," said Keeah.

"And their big, bad friend," said Julie.

Amid the swarm of flying wolves Gethwing flapped slowly on his ragged wings, closing the distance inexorably between him and the friends. His red eyes seethed with anger.

Urik nudged Galen, and together they sent a multicolored blast of sparks at the oncoming swarm. The wolves dispersed for a moment, then resumed their pursuit.

"We shall outrun them!" said Sparr. "We must get to the moon before the dragon. His wheel of life must be halted!"

The chariot sped ahead, but no matter how much the sorcerer and his mother urged the silver horse, the beasts continued to gain on them.

"Children, help me take the reins," said Max. "Wizards, fire. Slow him down. Take him out!"

Round after round of sizzling blasts exploded at the moon dragon, wounding him. At the same time, the chariot entered the darkening clouds, higher and faster toward the silver orb of the moon.

Time after time Gethwing faltered and dropped back, but each time he shook the blasts off and quickly regained his speed.

Because he's immortal, thought Eric.

With a few deft moves, Max and the children were able to land the chariot roughly on the silver plains. The horse galloped onward without a stop.

"Remember what Ko said about traveling to the Cave of Night," said Keeah.

"I remember," said Julie.

"The trick is knowing where to start," said Galen. "There is a statue of Gethwing in the easternmost range of blue mountains. We start there!"

The chariot roared into the blue mountains. Finding the statue of the evil dragon towering over a dark valley, the four children recited what the beast emperor had said.

"East beyond the light, west behind the shadow, north of the farthest valley, south of the tallest peak. . . ."

The chariot and its crew thundered across the icy plains, turning and racing, mile after mile, until south of the tallest of the blue mountains they spied a patch of ominous darkness among the jagged ledges.

Gethwing's secret lair, the Cave of Night.

The children tugged hard on the silver horse's reins. The chariot slid to a halt outside the black cave.

"The moon dragon has nearly landed!" said Max, looking back. "And his flying wolves are still with him!"

"Children, enter the cave," said Galen. "Find the dragon's wheel of life while the moon still shines. Dawn approaches in less than an hour. My brothers and I — and my mother — will take up the battle!"

The slowly brightening skies erupted with Gethwing's howling even before he set his feet on the icy ground.

"Eric, take the Medallion," said Zara.

"And my sword," Sparr added, and he tossed it high.

Eric grabbed both tight and discarded Ungast's lesser blade. "Thank you."

Neal, Keeah, and Julie entered the jagged arch of the cave's mouth. Darkness surrounded them.

All Eric heard were the age-old words of Gethwing's prophecy.

Five shall pass away, four shall wear the crown, three shall fall, two shall rise together, and one . . .

"Eric?" Keeah said.

Turning once before plunging in after his friends, Eric saw Urik embrace his family, then stand firm. The moon hung in the sky even as the sun began its rise.

"Eric, come," said Keeah, pulling him into the mouth of the cave. "We need you. No one more than you."

He gripped the sword, took her hand, and followed her into the darkness.

arc tome," said Keah, pulling him into
the mouth of the cave. "I need you. No one
more than you.
    He gripped the wand, took her hand, and
followed her in.

Twelve

The Long Story

The Cave of Night was a filthy darkness, thick
and heavy with the smell of burning.

No more than five feet inside the
entrance, the passage turned and became
impossibly narrow and close. More than
once Eric felt as if his breath was stopped in
his throat.

Which was not a bad thing, as the air was
damp with age and despair and the unmistakable smell of something dead.

"This is different from my vision," said Neal,

his voice sounding thin and small. "Way colder and creepier."

"That's because this is real," said Keeah. "Visions are just that, visions. Real is real."

Eric recalled his vision of a golden future, knowing that, like Neal's vision, it was not real, either. He brushed it from his mind.

Gethwing's prophecy is being fulfilled now.

This moment.

There is only this moment.

In they went among the cold rocks, drawn by the sound of stone grinding stone. It was Gethwing's wheel of life.

"Look!" said Julie. "There's something on the tunnel floor."

Eric flicked his fingers, and a spark flared in the air. Before being extinguished, its reflection flashed on the floor up ahead.

"A pool," he said. "Water."

All things connect . . .

The children crowded around, and the water became translucent. Images swam across its surface.

The great world of Droon, every acre, every square mile was spread out in a panorama of darkness and fire.

"This is Demither's doing," said Keeah. "She's telling us that time has run out."

The roofs of Jaffa City flamed with red and green fire, and the stones of its great palace rang with the assault of thousands of beasts.

Towers crumbled. Bridges fell. Water from a broken seawall flowed through the streets.

They saw Queen Relna run across the battlements, a colored staff high above her head. King Zello tripped backward up circular steps toward her, his twin clubs flailing, while dozens of lion-headed beasts pursued him.

"Lumpies, to the walls!" the king shouted.

"The Lumpies are gone!" came the queen's response. "Lost in the battle —"

"Not the Lumpies!" said Julie. "That means they never made it to the Bangledorn Forest."

Flames engulfed the royal palace's giant tower, and the children saw for the first time how the tower was positioned in the exact center of the city. The walls surrounded it in an almost perfect circle. It reminded them of the strange spoked circle sketched on Galen's old map.

Eric gasped. "It's like . . . a wheel."

"Droon's wheel of life!" Neal said. "In my vision of the future, Zabilac — I mean old Zabilac — told me that Droon had a wheel of life. It's right under Jaffa City. And the palace tower is its axle! If the tower falls, the wheel stops!"

Tears ran down Keeah's cheeks and fell into the pool, sending deep ripples across the surface and dispelling its terrifying scene.

She turned, her face tight with sorrow and anger. "Stop Gethwing's wheel. If it's the last thing we do —"

But when they entered the innermost cave, they discovered that the dragon's wheel of life was far more enormous than they had imagined. A giant flat disc nearly the entire size of the chamber swept around a central axle, and the sound of its turning was like a voice repeating *Doom, doom, doom, doom. . . .*

There were seven different-sized handprints placed equidistantly around the wheel.

And there were words.

Eric recited the prophecy from memory.

"Five shall pass away, four shall wear the crown, three shall fall, two shall rise together, and one . . . Gethwing told me the *five* meant the five cycles of Droon's millennial calendar that passed since his birth. . . ."

"What if the four with crowns is, you know, us?" asked Neal. "We're kind of like royalty. Keeah's already a princess. I'm the genie king. Julie's always been the Oobja princess. And, well, you're one of Zara's sons. Which I still can't believe."

"If we're the *four* wearing the crown," Julie said, "who are the three who fall?"

Eric frowned. "Salamandra was bothering me before about different people understanding prophecies differently. You know how strange she is. But maybe she was trying to tell me something."

"If the three are not Gethwing's enemies," said Keeah, "maybe they're our enemies. Gethwing and Ko. And, for sure, Neffu!"

"Then which two rise together?" Eric asked.

"This math is making my head hurt," said Neal, gazing at the moving stone. "But the number we need to add up to right now is seven. The wheel has seven handprints around its outside edge. We're only four. I'm going to guess and say that the other hands belong to Galen, Sparr, and Urik. I'm getting them —"

Neal ran to the mouth of the cave, where there was a muffled noise, then the clashing of blades. Julie and Keeah shot to the entrance to see what had happened.

The moment Eric tried to join them, a great dark form crashed from the jagged ceiling, and he was thrown to the ground. When he struggled to his feet, the odor of dragon filled his nose.

"Ungast," said Gethwing, moving out of the shadows. "We are alone now. Come to me. I want to see the face of a traitor."

The word struck Eric like a blade.

So, Gethwing knows. Maybe he always knew. Maybe he lured me here. Maybe he'll try to destroy me right here and now.

"I said . . . *come!*"

As if a powerful hand had grabbed his arm, Eric was dragged across the floor and dumped at Gethwing's feet.

"As I suspected. You are no longer my Prince Ungast," the dragon said, gazing at him. "You are merely . . . *him* . . . again."

Struggling, Eric stood up straight, his hand gripping Sparr's sword, and he realized he was thinking of what Keeah had said.

No one more than you.

"Yeah, I'm Eric Hinkle. And glad to be," he said, tossing his dark helmet to the ground.

"No matter," said Gethwing softly. "The bracelet keeps you in my control."

"The bracelet?" said Eric. And the moment he sought to remove the stony black hoop from his arm, he found he could not. It seemed to have fused with his skin.

"Two shall rise together," said the dragon. "You see, we did rise together. I had such hopes for you. Alas, you betrayed me. Even so, you will do my will."

"I won't . . . ," Eric said, but he could not move. His sword remained frozen at his side.

Gethwing grinned coldly. "You asked before about the *one*. The prophecy shall now be fulfilled. On the very hour of Jaffa City's fall, it happens."

Eric's heart skipped. "What happens?"

Gethwing took a breath. "*One shall stand in the ashes and never see the end of days.* There. Now you know. Look there. These words were inscribed on that stone the night of my birth. These are the words that govern me. That govern Droon."

The great wheel turned and turned, and at its very center, around the axle's point, deep marks were carved into the stone.

"Where are the ashes?" Eric demanded, recalling the ashes he had seen on his flight on the dragon's back so many hours ago. "Where are your ashes?"

"Behold!" Gethwing said. With a flick of his claw upward, the ceiling of the cave opened, and a bold silver light fell directly on the stone.

Gethwing stood, full of his own power, and put his arm into the moonlight. His scaly flesh began to burn with a silver flame.

"Look! Look, Eric Hinkle! I burn, yet I do not die! The prophecy is fulfilled! I have conquered. Jaffa City falls even as I speak. Now, do what you must do! Destroy your friends! You — have — no — choice! Do it. Now!"

At that instant, Keeah, Julie, and Neal reentered the cave, and Eric felt himself turn toward them and raise his sword.

"No . . . no!" he said. "I won't. I —"

One step, another, another. He struggled against the dragon's will, but could not resist it.

"Eric —" Keeah said, raising her hands.

The cave floor quaked suddenly, dust fell from the ceiling, and the jagged walls exploded.

All at once, Emperor Ko appeared.

Behind him stood a battalion of green-skinned goblins, armed and standing at attention.

Salamandra sidled up to Ko, her thorny hair coiling in tangles and lit with green fire.

"You!" gasped Keeah. "What —"

"I told you Ko needed to be here," Salamandra said. "It's all part of the prophecy. I'm sorry we're late for the get-together. I had . . . stuff to do. Catch me up?"

Ko roared. "Queen Salamandra rescued me from the Underworld and death. Now my goblins will destroy you all — you, too, moon dragon, *and your stone wheel* — and as the prophecy states, *I* will take my rightful place. If *one shall never see the end of days*, that one is me!"

"You lie!" Gethwing boomed.

In the standoff, Eric noticed something odd about one of the goblins behind the emperor.

Dangling from the goblin's shoulders, amid the knobs and bumps of green skin and bone, were golden threads, coiled and shiny.

Braids? thought Eric.

Then it came to him. The goblin was wearing tassels on his shoulders. Across the length and breadth of Droon, Eric had seen such tassels only once. On the shoulders of a friend.

Khan! King of the Lumpies! But how —

Then farther back in the distance, he spotted Jabbo. The pie maker's apron was stained with berry juice, and his paws were dusted with flour. Was he working *with* Salamandra?

Eric's mind flashed, and his heart leaped.

Jabbo's pies! They turn people into goblins. Salamandra asked him to bake pies to turn the Lumpies into goblins! They weren't lost! Salamandra brought them here! She hasn't betrayed us. There is hope after all —

With a single swift move, Eric struck the bracelet with the side of Sparr's sword. The bracelet fell to the cave floor.

"Goblins, attack!" boomed Ko.

"Attack?" said the goblin with shoulder tassels. "You want us to attack?"

"My commands are law!" shouted Ko.

"All righty, then," said Khan. "Boys?"

And the entire army of goblins rushed at Ko from behind, kicking him directly into Gethwing. The two beasts went at each other like a world at war. The cave thundered from wall to wall. Stone dust covered everything.

"To the wheel!" shouted Keeah.

The children leaped to the giant stone disc, and Eric felt magic flow in him as he touched its rough surface. "Galen! Urik! Sparr!"

The cave entrance blasted loudly, and the wizards, Max, and Kem streamed in. As one, Galen, Urik, and Sparr added their hands to the wheel.

The stone wheel began to slow.

"NEVER!" bellowed Gethwing. He pummeled Ko on the back and tore away from the emperor. Then he slammed his claws on Galen's shoulders and tossed him down.

Without every hand upon the wheel, it began to gain speed as before.

"He'll win!" cried Sparr. "Stop him! Urik, Mother, with me! We must stop Gethwing!"

"No!" cried Max. "Do not release your hold on the wheel. Do not lift your hands away!"

As if his entire life had led to this one moment, Max yanked Sparr's sword from Eric's belt and leaped at the dragon.

He wrapped his legs around Gethwing's neck and brought the flat of the blade down on the beast's head, battering him again and again, yelling at the top of his lungs.

"Leave him! Leave him! Leave him —"

Enraged, Gethwing tried to push Max off, but the spider troll would not be thwarted. He kept bashing the dragon's head as Gethwing stormed around the cave. Finally, the moon dragon was forced to drop Galen.

"Ha!" Max cried. He leaped away, and Zara, Urik, and Sparr together blasted the dragon to the ground.

They did the same with Ko, and Khan and his Lumpies bound the emperor and Gethwing with chains of magic thorns, courtesy of Salamandra.

As soon as Galen's fingers were back on the wheel, it slowed once more. When he faltered, Max was there to keep the old wizard's hand firmly on the stone.

Gethwing collapsed under the weight of Salamandra's thorny chains and began to choke as the wheel ground more slowly.

"It's happening!" said Keeah.

The longer they held the wheel, the slower it turned, and the more Gethwing suffered.

As the stone wheel slowed to nearly nothing, Eric could not take his eyes off the dragon. Gethwing's immortality was draining away from him. The moon dragon was dying right before their eyes.

His giant lungs heaved, his massive limbs twitched and shuddered less and less. At last, Gethwing went still.

The cave mouth rustled with a sudden flutter of wings, and Urik's three birds flew in, calling out tidings of peace.

"The beast armies have sensed their leader is defeated!"

"King Zello's forces have turned them back. Jaffa City's tower has fallen, its rubble hidden by flames and smoke. But the beasts are gone!"

"The war is over! It is over! Over!"

Eric's heart quaked to hear that the tower had fallen. As the axle of Droon's wheel of life, it meant the wheel was stopped.

Droon was finished.

He knew then that their final quest was over, too. It was the moment of peace in Droon. The moment that signaled the end of war, the end of danger, and the fulfillment of the ancient prophecy.

"We . . . can't . . . ," he said. "We can't end it like this. Kill Gethwing? We cannot kill. We *do* not kill. If we do, we're no better than beasts ourselves."

The wheel turned as slowly as possible without stopping completely.

Urik locked eyes with Galen, then with Sparr, and one by one they let go of the wheel.

Gethwing coughed, his eyelids flickered.

"The unbreakable bond," said Zara. "Sons, with me." Using their combined powers, the Queen of Light and her three powerful sons bound Gethwing together with Ko in adamantine chains that shimmered in every color of the rainbow.

"They cannot be breached or broken," Sparr said.

"Eric, you have spoken well," said Galen. "Few might have been as kind. Or as just."

"You would have been," said Eric. "Galen, you taught us what justice is, exactly as your mother taught you and Sparr and my great-great-great grandfather Urik."

"Before we get all mushy here, can we get out of this cave?" asked Neal. "It's giving me the creeps."

Eric smiled at first, but then his smile faded. *Even the creeps. We'll miss them, too.*

"Where does our quest take us now?" asked Max.

Home, thought Eric. *The quest is done.*

"I know," said Julie. "To the land of the lost. To Agrah-Voor."

Agrah-Voor. How long ago the children had visited the famed underground city! It was the domain of ghosts, where every fallen hero throughout Droon's long history waited for the coming of peace.

"I knew we'd see it," Julie said. "I knew we'd go there one last time."

One last time.

The words drained all the fire from Eric's heart. He knew that even in the victory of good over evil, their time in Droon was ending. The final quest was just that. Final. Finished. And the long story was over.

A few hours later, they were back in Droon, watching the city of Agrah-Voor from the vantage of its highest wall. Shago, their longtime friend and master thief, stood with them, tears in his eyes, as did the ghostly city's diminutive ruler, Queen Hazad.

The giant gates were flung wide, and the streets of Agrah-Voor emptied of centuries and thousands of its fallen heroes.

At the same time, its walls were filled to overflowing with every manner of evil beast known in Droon. All the attacking armies, the lion-headed beasts, the snakelings, the wingwolves, the wraiths — all of them were impelled through the ancient city's gates.

Gethwing and Ko squabbled and bickered

when they were thrown inside the impenetrable walls with their innumerable yet powerless forces. Princess Neffu, newly captured in Doobesh, was tossed kicking and screaming and ranting among the rest.

"Just wait!" she snarled.

"We will," said Sparr. "And so will you!"

"Unable to leave, you will live together below the surface of our land," said Galen. "And that may prove punishment enough."

Once all the beasts were inside, Zara, Galen, Urik, and Sparr clasped their hands together, and stone arches shot up over the city walls, joining one another and crisscrossing the city, sealing it forever from the outside.

"Ghosts, follow me," Queen Hazad said, "and enter the long-awaited daylight."

The moment the ghosts streamed into Droon's daylight, daylight entered them, too. With every step, Droon's fallen heroes took substantial form and walked among the living, with them, like them, and fallen no more.

And not only did daylight shine on them. For the moon still beamed, its silver rays blending with the golden streams of dawn.

Two shall rise together! The sun and moon.

A moment of quiet seemed to settle everything in its place, and Eric turned to the thorn queen, who had been watching silently with Jabbo at her side.

"Salamandra," he said, "you helped Galen, then betrayed us, then you betrayed Ko. Are you good or not?"

The thorn queen's thin lips grew into a broad smile. She pointed to her head. "Do you think I wear my hair this tangled because it looks good? My thoughts are as split as these ends. And as snarled."

"The ancient prophecy?" said Keeah.

"That thing?" The thorn queen laughed. "It's as ancient as last Tuesday. I just went back in time and delivered it to Gethwing's folks the day he was born. Simple. But fun."

"But what does it really mean?" asked Max.

Salamandra turned to Queen Zara. "Ask her. She's the one who sent it to me in a dream."

Queen Zara bowed. When she raised her head, her face seemed as youthful as it had been on that night so long ago on the outskirts of Pesh, when Eric had first seen her.

"In its words is one last secret, whose time has not yet come."

Eric breathed in. "And *Reki-ur-set*? It was the word that led me to Urik. Because of you, Salamandra, I found my family."

The thorn queen smiled at him. "Then my work here is done. By the way, Galen, I hope I get a mention in your *Chronicles of Droon*."

Galen laughed, too. "You are one of its main characters!"

"You see?" Salamandra said. "That's all I'm asking. Catch you later. Or maybe before!"

With that, a little storm of thorns grew up around her, and she was gone, leaving Jabbo to return to Doobesh in victory.

"Salamandra has done much mischief in her time, and performed many dark works," said Queen Zara. "But perhaps she has made amends. After all, she was as close to the beginning of our Droon adventure as anyone."

When they all returned to Droon's surface, Zara, true to her name as Queen of Light, lit a single tiny candle. Even under the combined sunlight and moonlight, the candle flared with a strong silvery light.

"And there it is," said Neal. "The last image from my vision of the future."

The candle's glow bathed the friends for a silent moment, then Zara tossed the candle high with a loud whoop.

Instantly, whatever black skies lingered across Droon brightened. The heavy clouds over the Dark Lands diminished until they were no more than a frail vapor. Together golden sunlight and silver moonlight shone over every inch of the land.

"Peace," said Galen softly. "Droon is finally at peace."

And another light flashed and twinkled on the far horizon.

"The rainbow staircase," said Neal, choking up. "Somehow I feel this is . . . this is . . ."

"Over?" whispered Julie, her eyes moist.

"The end?" said Keeah, turning to Eric.

Eric felt too full to speak. It was a great ending, and it had happened the way he had always hoped it would. Peace and light covered the land from sea to sea.

But it was an ending.

And his heart was breaking.

"Droon," he said. And then again. "Droon . . . Droon . . ."

There was nothing more to say. In that single word, life seemed to have come full circle for him. He expected to wake up any moment and run down the stairs to welcome Neal.

He would head through the kitchen, but this time his mother would not give him garbage bags to clean the basement. Or if she did, the basement would be just that. A basement.

Not an entrance to the most amazing experi-
ence in his life.

Every moment of their time in Droon came
back, memory rushing upon memory, until he
could barely breathe. He knew that all too
soon the image of Keeah, her long blond hair,
her blue tunic, the light in her eyes, would fade
like a dream upon waking.

"I guess we should go," he said. "Our parents will want us back."

"Funny," said Neal. "The more I look? That
light over there doesn't look much like the
rainbow staircase."

Eric started to turn toward the distant east,
but the three birds were suddenly there again,
flying frantically overhead.

"What is it, friends?" Urik asked.

"Jaffa City!" said Otli.

"The battle smoke has cleared!" Motli said.

"The tower stands!" said Jotli.

"Droon's wheel of life rolls on!" cried
Keeah.

"And that light still doesn't look like the staircase," said Neal.

Eric squinted, trying to get a better view of the light flickering over the far hills. Neal was right. It was unlike any he had seen. It was both distant and constant. It was less like a rainbow than a glimmer of gold.

"Then what exactly *is* it?" asked Julie, tugging the silver telescope from Neal's turban and scanning the horizon.

A gasp of breath came from the three sons of Zara at the same time.

"You can't be serious!" said Galen.

Sparr laughed brightly. "A joke perhaps?"

"The first of the legendary Seven Cities of Gold!" said Urik. "In my wanderings in Droon I learned of them. I even drew a map!"

Eric jumped. "*You* drew that map? The map Thog found in the Castle of Zorfendorf?"

Urik burst into laughter. "Zorfendorf! That's one of the funny names I made up to call myself!"

Galen laughed. "Well, Prince Urik Zorfendorf of Stars! The Seven Cities of Gold is a legend that goes back to the very beginnings of Droon. Once light returns to the Dark Lands, the golden cities will finally appear. Traveling there is said to be the greatest of all adventures!"

The horizon glowed more brightly with each passing moment.

"Even in the Upper World, we heard about the Seven Cities," said Zara. "They are supposed to be more beautiful than one can ever imagine."

"I want to go to there," said Neal.

"Oh, you will, my genie friend," said Sparr. "You will —"

"You mean it's *not* over?" asked Eric. "We haven't just ended the final quest?"

"Quest? Over?!" said Max, jumping up. "Anywhere else, perhaps. But this is Droon, and Droon is an endless voyage of discovery! And we need no prophecy to tell us that!"

Smiling, Zara placed her hand on Eric's shoulder. "The final secret of Gethwing's prophecy. I was talking about Droon when I said that *one shall rise from the ashes and never see the end of days*. Besides, Eric, you had a vision of this, did you not?"

Eric felt his heart leap into his throat. "I did. I sure did!"

"And now we see how visions become real," Urik said. "Pilkas, anyone?"

"Quill, finish up your scribbles and come!" said Galen. "There are more stories to write."

The magic feather pen scratched a word on a long scroll he was working on. "That should do it for now," he said in a squeaky voice. He leaped into Galen's saddlebag.

Eric picked up Quill's scroll, unrolled it, and read its very first words. At first, tears came to his eyes. Then he couldn't help but laugh. "I don't believe it!"

"Read it," said Keeah, mounting Leep, her shaggy white steed.

"It's a long story," said Eric.

Neal laughed. "That's the best kind," he said. "Besides, we have time. All the time in the world."

"In both worlds," said Queen Zara.

The friends jumped onto their pilkas and turned to the east, where the first of the Seven Cities of Gold glimmered under the rising sun.

Eric unrolled the scroll, cleared his throat, and began to read.

"'Eric Hinkle ran past his mother on the way through the kitchen . . .'"

Bagpipes and drums and the birdlike tweeting of flutes started up. They were soon joined by a trio of real songbirds, Urik's feathered friends, as they circled overhead.

"And we're off!" chittered Max.

And so, true to Eric's vision at last, the friends set off together toward the rising sun and Droon's ever-beckoning horizon.

.... = Border of
Dark Lands

17

19

33

32

34

Longbeard

A GUIDE TO DROON

A journey to help his village. A quest to save the Kingdom.

Out of the darkness, heroes will rise...

Also Available:

by Kathryn Huang

by Kathryn Huang & Kathryn Lasky

Read them all!

SCHOLASTIC

www.scholastic.com/gahoole

GAHOOLE15

THE SECRETS OF DROON

By Tony Abbott

An epic journey—and an incredible series!

Read them all!

■SCHOLASTIC

www.scholastic.com/droon

DROON36:8